Beauty In Battles

Rotanya Hargrove

Rotanya Hargrove

NY Publishers

LCCN: 2025924775

ISBN: 978-1-964365-48-0

Dedication

To Myself

To the woman I once was — thank you for surviving. You didn't give up, even when no one saw your tears. To the woman I'm becoming — keep rising. You are proof that broken things can still be breathtaking.

To Those Who Carried Me

To my family, my tribe, my day-ones — thank you for standing when I couldn't. Your love became my light in the darkest hour. This book exists because you believed I still could.

Acknowledgment

To my children and family — my heart, my strength, my reason. Your love gave me the will to fight, the courage to heal, and the purpose to keep going. You stood by me when I was broken and reminded me I was still whole. This is for you. This story — our story — is a love letter to the strength we share.

To the firefighters who pulled me from the rubble, your hands were God's hands that day.

To the women who've ever had to rise from ashes, whispering, "Not today" — I see you. This is for every woman who has had to rebuild herself from the ground up. Let these pages remind you: your brokenness was never the end — it was the beginning.

Table of Contents

About the Author

Rotanya Hargrove is a mother, a mogul, a miracle in motion. Born in the fire of the 1970s, she became a mother at just 15, learning how to raise a child while still becoming a woman herself. Life didn't hand her ease — it handed her grit. She faced heartbreak, divorce, and moments of deep loss that could have swallowed her whole. But instead of folding, she fashioned her pain into purpose.

After surviving a catastrophic building collapse that left her buried alive for six hours, Rotanya didn't just recover — she redefined herself. With legs crushed, her faith tested, and her future uncertain, she rose again — bolder, softer, wiser, and unstoppable.

She is the founder of Hotties Boutique, a body-positive fashion brand dedicated to helping women look good, feel good, and do good. Her impact is more than business — it's a legacy. A girl's girl. A hot girl. An it-girl. A soul that radiates truth.

This is her first memoir — a testimony to survival, faith, and feminine fire. Her story doesn't ask for pity. It demands praise — not for what she's endured, but for what she's becoming.

*Tanya with her 4 children – Tamel, Dazjohn, Ebony, & Emani,
and her fur baby – Nyla*

Tanya's parents – Gloria & Roosevelt

This is a true story of Grit, Glamour, and Glory!

I wasn't just built for battles — I was built to win, to shine, and to leave a trail of fire wherever I go. God didn't just save me — He made me unforgettable.

I'm not just a survivor — I'm a blueprint. Beauty, brilliance, boldness, and battle scars all coexist in me. I have been crushed and cracked but not erased.

When I walk into a room, I don't just turn heads — I shift energy. Because what I carry isn't just charm or style — it's power, purpose, and a presence rooted in resilience.

I'm not here to be liked — I'm here to be felt!

Behind every smile, every strut, every laugh, is a woman who fought through betrayal, heartbreak, near-death, and still chose to smile.

Beauty In Battles isn't just my story of surviving — it's about how I made survival look damn good.

Prologue

Tanya never expected her life to be divided by one violent, unspoken moment.

She was doing what women do — multitasking, managing, moving through life's chaos with quiet strength. Then, the world shifted. In seconds, the building she stood in became her grave.

Concrete roared. Walls caved. Screams vanished beneath dust. And then — silence.

Buried beneath slabs of debris, Tanya waited. Not for rescue. For breath. For God.

Time disappeared. She couldn't tell if she had been down there for minutes or days. Only her heartbeat—defiant, aching, alive—told her she hadn't become one more forgotten body in the news.

Six hours later, she was pulled from the rubble — battered, broken, but breathing.

But surviving wasn't the miracle. Becoming was.

This memoir is not about falling. It's about what happens after the fall — when you're left with nothing but faith, fear, and the faint memory of the woman you used to be.

Beauty in Battles is the story of a young woman's unrelenting will to live, lead, and love herself back together. It's the story of a mother who turned trauma into testimony, and a survivor who made recovery look radiant.

It's not about having it all together.

It's about finding beauty in the parts that broke.

And learning that rising isn't just possible — it's a calling.

Part I: Rooted & Ruptures

1. Morgan Avenue to Motels

In the quiet, tree-lined corners of Poughkeepsie, New York, in the 1970s, a girl named Tanya was born into a world already heavy with struggle.

Back then, the pastel-painted houses and cracked sidewalks couldn't hide the battles taking place behind closed doors—especially not in her own home.

Tanya had always known the comforting embrace of Poughkeepsie, New York, where the air was thick with the scent of fresh-cut grass, and the laughter of children echoed down Morgan Avenue.

Tanya – 9 years old

Growing up on this family-oriented block, she spent countless days playing with her stepdad's friends' children, the kids in the neighborhood, and her loyal dog Pepper, racing alongside them like a fuzzy shadow.

They were neighborhood friends—part of a close-knit group of kids who spent their days playing tag, hide-and-seek, going to the movies, bowling, and doing the usual preteen things.

Among them was a boy named Ebony, a soft and kind presence Tanya admired from the start. He was a few years older—14 when she was just 11—which kept their connection in the safe, platonic space of childhood friendship. Still, Tanya and Ebony had always liked each other, and as the years passed, that friendship deepened.

The world felt safe and predictable, a tapestry woven from the bonds of community, where every adult was a friend, and every child was a playmate.

But that idyllic childhood began to unravel in the early 1980s when the dark specter of drugs crept into their small town.

Tanya hadn't been 12 yet, but she had already seen more than most people twice her age. Her mother, once the most beautiful woman she knew, had fallen deeply into the grip of drugs. The home was loud some nights and eerily silent others.

She often cried herself to sleep, praying that tomorrow would be different—that her mother might look at her again the way she used to, with love instead of fog.

Tanya watched as her once-vibrant home transformed into a place overshadowed by substance abuse. Her stepdad, who had always been the life of the block, gradually succumbed to the bottle, leading to a fateful night that would change everything.

One evening, after a long drinking binge, he got into a fight with some local boys. Tanya remembered the chaos vividly, the shouts and the sounds of fists connecting with flesh, culminating in her stepdad collapsing to the ground.

The image of him lying there, vulnerable and hurt, was etched into her mind as he was rushed to the hospital, where he would remain for nine long months. When he finally came home, he wasn't the same man.

The injury had left him nearly brain-dead, and the vibrant laughter that once filled their home was replaced by a heavy silence.

Time, however, as its nature is, didn't stop. It kept crawling, and soon, Tanya was celebrating her 13th birthday. By this time, she had started dating Ebony.

Ebony would walk her to and from school, they'd spend hours talking on the phone, and often grab Chinese food or pizza together. Their bond grew stronger over time.

When Ebony and his father weren't getting along, Tanya would even sneak him in through her bedroom window so he'd have a place to stay. Ebony was raised by his father, Peter—a tall, dark, hardworking, intelligent, and deeply religious man who took on the responsibility of raising his three sons alone after their mother left.

Despite the gloomy and depressing environment at home, Tanya found solace in the company of her sweetheart, Ebony. They would soothe each other and stay committed to their relationship, regardless of what others thought or said.

But not everyone approved. The older girls in the neighborhood didn't like Ebony dating Tanya. They whispered that she was too young for him, casting side-eyes and making her feel like she didn't belong.

Ebony, trying to navigate both loyalty to his community and his feelings, even dated other girls for a time—short flings meant to appease the pressure. But no matter how far he strayed, he always found himself back at Tanya's doorstep, trying to win her over again. There was something about her—her quiet strength, her honesty, her rawness—that kept pulling him in.

Their connection ran deeper than curiosity or rebellion. It was innocent and sensitive before it was ever physical. Their bond felt more rooted in love and emotional survival than anything else. It wasn't about rushing to grow up—it was about clinging to each other in a world that was already demanding they be grown.

Tanya's mother, overwhelmed by the changes and the constant strain of caregiving, began to withdraw. Their family fractured under the weight of desperation, and soon, they—Tanya's mom and stepdad—split up.

With her mother unable to cope, their lives spiraled into chaos, leading them to live in motels far from the warmth of Morgan Avenue.

Though Tanya was only 13, she felt the weight of the world on her shoulders. Her older siblings, caught up in their own lives, drifted away, leaving Tanya and her little brother to navigate this new reality with their mother.

They shared cramped motel rooms, where the air was stale, and the walls felt like they were closing in. Yet, amidst the turmoil, Tanya clung to the love she had for her mother. They made do with what little they had, and her mother worked tirelessly to provide for them, ensuring they had the essentials—even if luxuries were a distant memory.

When they finally moved into a small apartment, Tanya felt a glimmer of hope. The walls were bare, but they were their own, and it felt like a fresh start.

It was during this time of rebuilding that her connection with Ebony grew even stronger. Tanya, carrying the weight of a broken home and the responsibility of a little brother, found relief in Ebony. He, in turn, found purpose in loving her. His smile lit up the dimmest of days of hers. And her hugs snatched away all his worries.

2. Love in the Eyes of Chaos

Love bloomed like flowers in the spring. Days seemed vibrant, and nights were moonlit. What began as a childhood friendship—running through the streets—gradually transformed into something more. Tanya found escape in that unexpected yet familiar place: in the eyes of Ebony. The boy who had always been there but now seemed to see her in a new light.

He made her feel seen and special, like she was more than the chaos surrounding her. Their relationship was still naïve, tender, and budding—but love, even young, has a power of its own.

Ebony was different from the boys she'd known on Morgan Avenue—not just in how he treated her, but in how he understood her. Kind, attentive, and grounded, he offered a safe space she hadn't known she needed. He was genuinely interested in her well-being.

Their desire blossomed gently, naturally, and swiftly, and Tanya found herself falling—really falling—deeply in love for the first time. Ebony became her refuge, a bright spot in the tumult of her life.

They spent evenings talking about their dreams and sharing their fears, building a bond that felt unbreakable and rooted in honesty and care. Tanya confided in him about her past, her struggles, and the pain of watching her family crumble.

To her surprise, Ebony listened without judgment—not with pity, but with understanding, wrapping, offering, and supporting like a warm blanket on a cold night.

As their relationship deepened, Tanya began to see glimpses of a future that didn't seem so bleak. She envisioned a life filled with laughter again, a home where love triumphed over adversity. With each conversation, Tanya began to imagine a life beyond her trauma—a future filled with possibility.

With Ebony by her side, she dared to dream of a world beyond the confines of her past—a world where she could rewrite her story, one filled with hope, resilience, and the promise of a brighter tomorrow.

Ebony helped her see that healing was possible, that love could be both gentle and strong. Together, they sketched out a vision of tomorrow where happiness returned, where suffering was acknowledged but not all-consuming.

Through the trials and tribulations, Tanya learned that while the past could not be changed, it didn't have to dictate her future. With each passing day, she grew more assertive and more determined to carve out a life that honored her journey while embracing the love that surrounded her.

In that small apartment filled with memories and dreams, Tanya began to write the next chapter of her life—one filled with love, healing, and the unwavering spirit of a girl who refused to let her circumstances define her.

3. From Pain to Power

With the chaos at home pressing down on both of them, Tanya and Ebony began dreaming of an escape. They planned it with the vision that it would set them free and make them happy. Soon, they started working on their plan, which was to have a baby together.

The two believed that if they had a child, they could qualify for assistance, get their own apartment, and finally be together as a family—independent and at liberty from the turmoil they each faced at home. As neither Tanya nor Ebony felt like they had space to breathe, much less grow.

In the haze of young love and fear, what they didn't fully understand yet was that bringing a baby into the world wouldn't just change their address—it would change everything.

They desperately wanted to be out of their complicated home lives. Tanya's mother was struggling with substance abuse, and Ebony's father ruled his home with iron expectations, strict and unyielding with his boys.

For years, they had danced at the edges of desire—close enough to feel its heat but never close enough to burn. They weren't physically intimate until Tanya was around 14. But when she was nearly 15, there was no more waiting.

The plan was in action, and every touch became a promise, and every embrace a vow. They loved fiercely, endlessly, as if the world outside their tangled sheets had ceased to exist. They had been having sex continuously since then.

At first, she didn't have the nerve to go through with it. But Ebony seemed sure. Many of the older guys in the neighborhood were already sexually active, and he felt anxious to keep up.

It was supposed to be the perfect day—school was out for summer break, and Ebony's dad was at work. He invited Tanya over, and they had planned to take that next step in their relationship. They tried, but Tanya couldn't handle the pain and asked him to stop. And he did.

Ebony was visibly upset—not at her, but with himself. He didn't have much experience either and was feeling the pressure.

But once the dam between them broke, it became a relentless tide. From that moment on, they were consumed—

not in fleeting moments of passion, but in an unbroken chain of desire, as inevitable as the turning of seasons.

Tanya was not even 16 years old yet when the world around her crashed again so very quickly. She found herself pregnant—the love (and the plan) was indeed powerful and had escalated severely. It wasn't that the baby was accidental, but the world was cruel.

Their plan took effect, and Tanya was expecting, but to the world, it was a baby out of wedlock! There was no celebration, no baby shower, just shame, judgment, and a feeling of being lost in a storm she couldn't stop.

She dropped out of school with tears in her eyes and a baby in her belly. But even at her lowest, she carried a quiet flame—a determination not to let her life be defined by pain.

Soon, she gave birth to a cute baby boy, Tamel. It was a bright day in April 1989. With her baby boy on her hip and resilience in her bones, she enrolled in the New York State GRASP Home Program.

Getting her GED wasn't easy, especially with diapers to change and bills to worry about, but she did it. She held that Document like it was a crown—proof that she hadn't been defeated.

Tanya celebrated her sweet sixteen alongside Tamel's 1st birthday, marking two milestones that felt both tender and surreal. Just a few years later, her 21st birthday would arrive hand in hand with another life-changing event—her wedding to Ebony.

By then, she had moved out of her mother's house, leaving behind the noise and unpredictability of her childhood home. She and Ebony had gotten their first apartment and had started living in it together.

In its place, she embraced the steady rhythm of a shared life, building something new—something hers—with the boy who had grown into the man she loved. Not long after, she learned that a live-in (which was no less like a marriage in her situation) was a new kind of challenge. Her husband had been raised in tradition—she became pregnant again, his voice became law, and his identity swallowed hers.

In June of 1991, when she was just 17 years old, Dazjohn arrived in her lap—her 2nd kid, another lovely baby boy.

Ebony and Tanya raised their sons with love, intention, and the quiet strength that comes from shared struggle, living together, and growing through life hand in hand.

Ebony was a mirror of his own father in many ways and was especially firm when it came to raising their boys. He believed in discipline, in lesson plans, and in education, not just as a requirement but as a tool for survival. He pushed them to be self-sufficient, to think beyond the classroom, and to embrace entrepreneurship—to have their own, build their own, and rely on no one but God and themselves—values he believed would prepare his children for the real world.

Tanya 21 & Ebony at 25

In 1994, Ebony made a life-changing decision. He joined the Nation of Islam under the guidance of Minister Louis Farrakhan, seeking deeper discipline and spiritual clarity. A step that would deepen the foundation of their family. Tanya embraced the journey alongside him.

The Nation of Islam became more than a spiritual anchor—it was the foundation upon which they built their family. Their commitment to the principles of Islam grew with time. They were active participants at their mosque in Albany, New York, attending weekly study groups, embracing their roles within the community, and frequently attending Muhammad Mosque number #7 in Harlem.

Ebony, now a registered member of the Fruit of Islam (FOI), immersed himself in discipline, obedience, and service. He sold newspapers, bean pies, and incense, learning to provide through self-reliance and spreading the teachings of the Honorable Elijah Muhammad.

Tanya, equally devoted, found sisterhood, growth, and her place within the MGT (Muslim Girls Training) and GCC (General Civilization Class), where she learned practical life skills and spiritual discipline. She was taught to cook, sew, nurture, and grow—not just as a woman, but as a Muslim woman walking a path of faith and purpose.

Guided by faith and duty, Ebony was told that to be in right standing with the Nation—and with Allah, that if he truly intended to live by the teachings of Islam, he would need to marry Tanya—the mother of his children, his partner in faith and life. It was the correct path, the righteous path.

Not just for appearances or tradition, but because it was the divine order of things. And so, he did. With quiet sincerity and deep love, Ebony proposed to Tanya. She was 5 months pregnant at that time with their 3rd child.

The two were married in a small, intimate ceremony at the local justice of the peace. There were no elaborate decorations or crowded pews—just the two of them, their boys, close friends and family, and members of their study group, and the presence of God.

4. The House Went Quiet

Tanya and Ebony's days were full, and their home was vibrant. Tanya glowed with life and love.

Through the years, the laughter of their children filled their home, memories settled into the walls like warm sunlight, and their journey—marked by struggle, devotion, and triumph—continued to unfold.

By 1996, they welcomed baby Ebony, their first daughter, into a home now deeply rooted in the core principles of Islam.

Together, they raised their family on the values of faith, self-discipline, love, and legacy. They attended Saviours' Day annually—traveling to Chicago every February 27, joining the sea of believers in celebration, reflection, and rededication.

Faith gave her grounding, but it also came with a heavy cloak of submission. As a wife, she was taught to listen, to obey, to follow. And she did, for years—speaking softly, dressing modestly, pouring herself into her family, working & raising her kids.

They made memories in their modest home, filled with the warmth of their growing children, the scent of home-cooked meals, and the hum of daily commitment. It wasn't always easy, but it was theirs, rooted in love, structure, and a shared dream of something better for their children.

Life continued to evolve for Ebony and Tanya, sometimes in ways they never expected.

It was around the same time that Ebony's mother reentered his life after years of distance, opening the door to long-lost connections and great wisdom. She had left him when he was just 3 years old.

Having been an active participant in the Nation of Islam for over fifty years, she carried with her the teachings, discipline, and deep history of the movement. She shared endless stories about the evolution of the Nation—its leaders, its values, and the spirit of its people.

Beyond her words, she brought warmth into their home through the food she taught them to make. She showed Ebony and Tanya how to bake the best bean pies, a cherished Native dessert they sold during the holidays, and how to craft a perfect lemon meringue pie—Tanya's favorite thing to make.

She also taught them to simmer Navy Bean Soup, "good for the soul," as she always said, filling the kitchen with comfort and purpose.

These recipes became more than meals; they became lessons in love and legacy—a skill and tradition they would later pass down for generations.

Through her, Ebony and Tanya were reunited with many brothers and sisters he had always known existed but hadn't truly known. It was a time of rediscovery, of expanding family and healing old spaces.

Their family was growing constantly. They visited Pittsburgh. They visited California. They visited Chicago, traveling and getting to know Ebony's siblings.

Tanya balanced the weight of it all with grace, holding down a steady job at IBM while still tending to the needs of their growing family. She worked hard, never missing a day, determined to build something stable after being a temp for four years. Ebony, meanwhile, worked as a barber, building a loyal clientele with his easy charm and skilled hands.

They were thriving and surviving in tandem, shoulder to shoulder, through the everyday challenges and quiet victories. Despite the demands of work and family, they carved out time for joy. There were family road trips to Pittsburgh, long weekends in Lake George, and heartfelt visits down South to North Carolina, where laughter echoed across porches and memories were made around kitchen tables. These getaways became sacred moments when time slowed down, and love stretched wide.

Through every twist in their journey, Ebony and Tanya remained rooted in each other. Life was not without chaos, but it was always full of purpose. Together, they created a home where family—by blood or by choice—was always welcome.

Life was no less than a struggle when they were met with another challenge. Though they accepted it and emerged conquering, Tanya's cousin Chrissy arrived at their doorstep, overwhelmed and desperate, carrying her infant daughter.

Without hesitation, Tanya and Ebony took the baby in, caring for her as their own while Chrissy disappeared to find her footing.

Days turned into weeks, and weeks into months—eight months, to be exact—before Chrissy would return. In that time, their home expanded with love and responsibility, as they raised yet another child in the rhythm of their household, never wavering in their commitment to family.

Tanya with her 4 children and her niece, Mena – Chrissy's daughter

During this time, she became pregnant with her 4th daughter and worked faithfully up until her ninth month—pushing through exhaustion, swollen feet, and long hours.

But just weeks before she was due, the company announced layoffs, and Tanya's position was among them. The news hit hard. After all that dedication, walking out of IBM for the last time felt like losing more than a job.

Tanya had barely crossed her teens when the world began demanding more of her than it ever should have of someone so young.

With two sons, two daughters tugging at her heartstrings, and a husband she still believed in—still loved with the eyes of the girl she once was—Tanya held her family together as best she could. The days blurred into one another, marked by diapers, dinners, and the delicate balancing act of maintaining harmony.

Not long after, Tanya landed another job. She got this job very outlandishly. Saint Cabrini Home—a court-ordered placement of boys and girls ages 12-21 who have committed crimes and/or were displaced.

One sunny afternoon, while attending a Family Day picnic at Saint Cabrini Home with her friend Berta for her daughter, Shy, who was in placement, something unexpected happened.

The air was filled with laughter, music, and the smell of grilled food and wet grass. The children chased bubbles, kids running through the lawn with face paint and ice cream, and families hugging after long separations.

Tanya had come to support Berta, sitting beneath a large oak tree, watching as Shy and the other children played games with their parents and caretakers. But before long, her gentle spirit drew others in.

She joined a group of girls playing double Dutch, her laughter blending with theirs as she jumped the rope like she was one of them.

Well along, one of the girls asked if she could braid her hair. Tanya beamed radiantly, sat her between her knees, and began parting and weaving her hair into two neat cornrows. Her fingers moved with both care and familiarity.

Soon, Shy and four of her friends gathered in a circle around her. They talked, laughed, played games, and shared stories, enjoying their time—Tanya asking them about studies, their dreams, and what they wanted to be. For a moment, all the walls that life had built around those girls seemed to fade.

Across the lawn, the sun began to set, painting the sky in orange and gold. What Tanya didn't realize was that the Deacon of the Home had been watching her from her office window the whole time. She saw the way Tanya connected with the girls—no judgment, no hesitation—just warmth and genuine care.

It was supposed to be a simple, peaceful day—a day of reunion and small joys. But as the afternoon unfolded, the universe had other plans.

She found herself at a crossroads—qualified, capable, but unsure of what came next, when, after the picnic wound down, the Deacon stepped outside and called her over.

She said to her, "I've been watching you from the window. The way you connect with them… It's special. If you ever need a job, come see me. I'll make sure you're hired."

Her eyes were following her all the time as she gently interacted with the girls. Tanya's presence was calm but firm, nurturing yet strong.

A week later, Tanya applied. And in 1998, her new chapter began at a place where girls found themselves tangled in the juvenile justice system.

Then onwards, the days belonged to her family. The mornings, to chores, errands, and motherhood. But it was the nights that demanded everything and that defined her. That's when she clocked in at her workplace.

Tanya didn't just show up for a paycheck—she showed up for the court-ordered, wounded, and often forgotten young women, who were both hardened and hurting.

When the house finally quieted, she would slip out the door and into the sterile stillness of Saint Cabrini Home, a lock-up facility for youth who had slipped through the cracks of the world but hadn't yet been swallowed by the system, created by Mother Cabrini.

There, she poured herself out, helping others while silently carrying the heavy, invisible weight of her own home on her back.

For 20 years, she worked the cottages—mostly with girls, though boys were housed there too. Twenty-two girls to a cottage, four cottages on the grounds, each its own universe of trauma, survival, and stubborn hope. Tanya was more than staff; she was a counselor, referee, mother figure, and mentor. She taught independent living skills in between breaking up fights, diffusing emotional storms, and helping these young women see themselves as more than just their mistakes.

Until this day, her favorites keep in touch with her, calling her for her birthday, checking up on her different milestones, and happenings.

Back home, Ebony stayed with the kids while she worked. He still had that boyish charm, the same crooked smile that had made her fall headfirst in love back in the days when they were just kids on Morgan Ave, full of big dreams and bigger hearts. He did his part—watching the children, warming bottles, pacing the floors during midnight cries.

And when morning came, Tanya would return, bleary-eyed but determined, and they'd switch roles like dancers in a tired duet. He'd collapse into bed, and she'd take on the day.

They were a team. Or at least, they tried to be.

But something had shifted. The silence of the long nights began to settle deep into Ebony's spirit. As the kids slept soundly in their beds and the soft flicker of the television danced across the walls of an empty room, a different kind of noise filled the room—one that couldn't be heard, only felt. Loneliness.

Lonesomeness crept in. Not the kind that meant he didn't love his family, but the kind that whispered doubts into the quiet. The kind that made him question if he was seen, if he mattered beyond being the man who kept the kids alive until Tanya returned.

And from that, a crack began to form, thin, barely noticeable at first. But all it takes is one fracture for everything to begin falling apart. That loneliness was a crack in the glass.

Eventually, someone stepped into that space—a woman who smiled at him like he wasn't invisible. In that moment, her attention felt like sunlight to a man who had been sitting in shadow for far too long. She smiled at Ebony like he wasn't unseen. Like he wasn't just someone else's husband or a stand-in father doing the graveyard shift at home. She looked at him as though he still held promise, still had light behind his eyes.

It started with casual conversations, then phone calls, then things he told himself didn't mean anything. But they did.

Soon, the truth came to light, and it crushed more than trust—it fractured the very foundation Tanya had been fighting to hold together. When she found out, it was like the air left her lungs.

She'd suspected it—the late-night phone buzzing, the sudden distance. But nothing prepares you for the moment your trust is shattered by the person you've built your life with.

The tears came slowly at first, as she held her kids in the hallway, watching Ebony try to explain away what couldn't be undone.

"I felt alone," he said, looking everywhere but at her. "I didn't mean for this to happen. I didn't think I mattered to you anymore."

Tanya's heart broke—not just from the betrayal, but from the realization that somewhere in the middle of surviving, they had both started sinking. She had been so focused on keeping the lights on, keeping their kids fed, keeping their lives moving—that she hadn't seen him drowning.

But pain doesn't erase love. And love doesn't erase pain. She didn't leave—not that night. Because something in her believed in the dream they once had, she prayed harder than ever, asking God to hold her together, to show her a way to rebuild what had been broken.

For the sake of their children, she stayed. For the sake of the family they promised to build, she forgave. But forgiveness came with its own weight... mornings felt different.

Tanya's smile was softer, and her guard was higher. She still kissed him goodbye, still tucked their kids in at night— but part of her was watching, waiting to see if he would do it again.

Ebony, on the other hand, felt guilt like a ghost haunting every quiet moment between them. He saw the way she looked at him now—not with anger, but with hurt. And that hurt cut deeper than any argument ever could.

They both tried. Family dinners. Long talks. Mosque on Sundays. Quiet prayers in separate rooms. They tried because they loved their babies. Because walking away felt like giving up on everything they had fought to create.

But the truth was—they were both scared. Scared that love might not be enough. Scared of failing their children. Scared of waking up one day and realizing they no longer recognized the people they had become.

Still, Tanya got up every night and went to work. Ebony stayed home, kissed their children goodnight, and tried to be better. Not perfect. Just better. Because love is not just what happens in the beginning—it's what you choose in the middle of the storm, when staying feels just as hard as leaving. And in the quiet of those long nights, as the boys slept and the house stood still, Tanya held on.

Not because she was weak. But because she still believed healing was possible. And sometimes, that belief is the bravest thing a woman can do.

Part II: Love, Losses & Loyalty

5. Love Wasn't Enough

Tanya's days were long and relentless: early mornings preparing meals, full-time shifts at Saint Cabrini Home in West Park caring for children who weren't hers, and late nights returning to her own.

She gave that job 20 years of herself—steady service, quiet love, and sacrifices no one ever saw. Her coworkers admired her strength, her poised calm in difficult moments. Yet behind the closed door of a bathroom stall or in the muted silence of her car, Tanya sometimes cried alone, overwhelmed but never defeated.

Even amid the whirlwind of motherhood and labor, she refused to let her dreams die. She enrolled at Ridley Lowell School for Business in Poughkeepsie, managing to steal hours between shifts and school pickups to invest in herself.

She dreamed of one day owning a business, of standing in a room not just as someone's wife or someone's mother— but as Tanya: the fighter, the survivor, the woman who never stopped becoming.

By the age of 26, Tanya was a mother of four—two boys, Tamel and Dazjohn, and two girls, Ebony and

Emani—and she believed she had the perfect family, one that mirrored the love she once saw in her husband's eyes. There were beautiful moments, no doubt. But there were shadows, too—lengthening with time, creeping into conversations, lingering in silence.

Eventually, that silence between them grew louder than any argument ever could. It was a stillness that screamed.

Tanya had always believed in second chances. She'd given Ebony one. Then another. And another after that.

She stayed up praying on nights she should've packed her things. She fought for their marriage like it was a war she was determined to win—for their children, for the family they'd built, for the version of love she'd always dreamed could survive anything.

But over time, the battlefield changed. She realized she was no longer fighting *with* Ebony. She was fighting *against* him.

The affairs didn't stop—not after the first time, or the fifth. Each time he swore, it was the last. Each time, she believed him a little less. Her trust became a threadbare cloth, full of holes and unraveling at the edges, yet she stretched it over a house filled with children who needed the illusion of wholeness.

And then came the betrayal that finally broke her.

He cheated with one of her brother's baby's mother, a woman Tanya had trusted around her children. A woman she had invited into her home. Had shared food, space, and civility with—for the sake of peace, for the sake of family.

It started with Tanya noticing the lingering looks, the sudden silences, the strange tension in the room whenever Ebony and her brother's baby's mother interacted. She couldn't ignore the shift—her instincts screamed that something wasn't right.

So, she confronted Ebony. Asked him straight out. And, of course, he denied it. Played it off like she was imagining things. Accused her of being insecure, jealous, and even paranoid.

But the truth has a way of showing itself.

One night, Tanya decided to go out with her friend Aja, trying to shake the heaviness from her chest. She needed a break, a distraction. Something that felt like freedom. But what she got was confirmation.

There they were—Ebony and the woman—posted up in the club like they had nothing to hide. Laughing. Drinking. Dressed alike like some twisted, public declaration. The kind of matching outfits that scream "we're together" without saying a word.

That was all Tanya needed to see.

She walked straight up to him and said, "You've got 15 minutes to get to the house and get your things. It's over."

He tried to backpedal. Called. Texted. Blew up her phone with promises, apologies, and tired declarations of love. *I want my family. I love my family. Let me come home.*

But Tanya was done.

The news hit like a wrecking ball. Not only had Ebony crossed the line—he set fire to it.

Tanya didn't cry this time. Not like before. No slumped shoulders. No shaking hands. Something inside her had already detached—quietly, steadily, over time.

Like her soul had finally accepted what her heart had been fighting to deny: that love should never come wrapped in betrayal. That forgiveness doesn't mean forfeiting your worth.

That night, while her children slept peacefully in the next room, Tanya sat alone in the living room. The stillness was loud, but she didn't flinch. She looked around the room she had held together with prayers and patience, and she whispered to herself: "I deserve more than this."

And for the first time, she truly meant it.

That night, Tanya looked around and realized she no longer recognized herself. She didn't know who she was anymore.

And that's when she made the hardest decision of her life: to leave.

She walked away not because she was bitter, but because her soul had gone quiet under the weight of titles, routines, and expectations.

Somewhere along the way, she had lost herself, and now she needed to remember.

Her marriage to Ebony spanned over 26 years. That's 26 celebrations, festivities, and mournings, 26 nights and mornings, 26 anniversary dinners—some filled with joy, others strained with silence. It was a lifetime of compromise, of keeping peace, of swallowing words.

There were soft moments and small battles, but mostly, there was a quiet erosion of her spirit.

Leaving the marriage wasn't about escape. It was about rediscovery. She walked out with no map—but with strength, with faith, with a light still flickering inside her, ready to catch flame. She left the marriage, but not her strength. Not her light.

Divorced, but not broken, Tanya rose from the ashes with a fire that had always been there—flickering beneath the surface, waiting for air.

Years passed. Ebony stayed in his new relationship. And eventually, the woman—Tanya's former friend, her brother's baby's mother—got pregnant again. This time, it was Ebony's baby she carried.

Now the woman who once shared Tanya's kitchen, who held her kids like family, had not only Tanya's niece and nephew… but her husband's child, too.

Tanya had known struggle. She had faced poverty, raised babies while still one herself, endured heartbreaks that bent her but didn't break her. She had been betrayed by people she loved, and she had watched pieces of her old self fall away—sometimes gently, sometimes violently. And yet, she stayed soft. She kept loving. Kept praying. Kept waking up every day and showing up—for her children, her work, and the dream of a life that still had color.

Now, when Tanya walks the streets of Poughkeepsie, she moves with a quiet grace—each step a symbol of healing. The city hasn't changed, but she has.

What once triggered pain now reflects her progress. Her story isn't rooted in what broke her. It's rooted in how she mended.

Piece by piece.

Day by day.

She didn't just survive—she softened, she opened, she bloomed.

And in that blooming, she found the woman she was always meant to become: grounded, glowing, and finally free.

6. Becoming Tanya Again

The days that followed her divorce were not gentle. Tanya was now a single mother of four—navigating the wreckage of a life she had poured herself into. For years, she had existed in roles assigned to her: wife, mother, peacemaker, survivor.

But now, with the silence of separation settling in, she had to ask herself: Who am I without him?

The answer didn't come all at once. It came slowly, through long nights and early mornings. Through meal prepping, school drop-offs, and quiet cries in the shower. She poured what little she had left into her children—and then, when they were safe and sleeping, she poured into herself.

She went back to school part-time. Picked up new classes in business and wellness, picked up extra shifts at work. She joined a gym, learned to cook for pleasure again, and started journaling.

Her body changed. Her thoughts sharpened. Her spirit lifted. And when she looked in the mirror, sadness no longer stared back. Instead, she saw a woman returning to herself.

She was becoming Tanya again.

Then he came. A New York State Trooper—tall, polished, clean-shaven, and quiet in the way that made you lean in.

He was married. She knew better. She *always* knew better. But he looked at her like she was whole, not broken. He made her laugh without trying. He listened—really listened—when she spoke.

He made her feel safe. Desired. Human.

She told herself it was just companionship. A few conversations. A little comfort. But comfort turned into lingering touches. Into long nights of confessions. Into moments where she forgot to guard herself.

It didn't last. It was never built to.

But when it ended, Tanya didn't crumble. She had already learned how to stand.

After everything she had endured with Ebony, Tanya finally stopped asking for the man she *wanted* and started praying for the man she *needed*.

Her prayers weren't loud or dramatic—they were quiet, whispered into the stillness of the night after the kids were asleep. After the dishes were done. After the noise of the day died down enough for her to hear the aching in her own heart.

"Ya Allah," she'd whisper. "Send me someone real. Someone smart. Someone who sees me beyond motherhood. A man who can protect me, provide for me, and pour into me as I've poured into everyone else."

That was when *Stylist* came walking into her life.

One ordinary afternoon, while running errands in sweatpants and a headscarf, barely a hint of lip gloss on, she met Stylist.

He was ten years younger, with a grin that could melt New York ice and a boldness that made her smirk. At first, she brushed him off.

"Boy," she said, laughing. "I have kids your age."

"I'm not a boy," he replied, locking eyes with hers. "I see a queen when I look at you."

Tanya rolled her eyes. But Stylist didn't fall away. He showed up—in texts, in phone calls, with iced coffee in hand and encouragement in his voice. He asked about her day. He remembered things she forgot she even told him. He told her she was glowing—even when she felt exhausted.

He wasn't what she expected—but somehow, he was everything she had asked for. Young. Fine. Sharp.

One day, against her better judgment, she said yes to a date. She didn't expect anything. But she fell—fast. Not just for Stylist, but for the way he saw her. As more than someone's mother. More than someone's ex-wife. More than a woman who'd carried too much for too long.

He saw her joy. Her fight. Her tenderness. And, for the first time in years, Tanya began to see it too.

Now, Tanya walks taller.

She still has four children. She still works long hours. Life isn't easy—but her soul is lighter. She doesn't carry bitterness for what was done to her. Instead, she carries gratitude for what she chose to do next.

And Ebony? He's out there—caught in the consequences of his own decisions. But Tanya doesn't curse his name. She thanks him. For the lessons. For the children. For the heartbreak that forced her back into herself.

Because sometimes, it's the deepest wounds that create the clearest openings.

And Tanya?

She's no longer just surviving.

She's finally living.

7. **What Being in Love Again Looked Like**

Tanya was in love again… With Stylist.

He had a hustle that kept money in his pockets and a strut that turned heads when he walked into a room. This wasn't Ebony-the-barber clocking in at the shop. No—Stylist's money was fast. Flashy. *Illegal.* And Tanya knew it. But she also knew how long it had been since someone made her feel *seen.*

He took her out to places she'd only double-tapped on Instagram. Bought her heels that came in red-bottom boxes. Sent her cash just because she made him laugh that day. But what shook her most wasn't the money—it was the *attention.*

He was into her. Not just her body. Not just because she had kids. He was into *Tanya.* Her mind. Her dreams. Her *fire.*

He listened. He showed up. He made her feel like a woman again, not just a mom on autopilot.

Eventually, they agreed to be official. But loving Tanya came with *layers.* Four children. Four unique personalities. A home that ran on routine, boundaries, and survival.

And Stylist? He didn't come with a manual. He had no experience with tantrums, homework drama, or teenage moods.

At first, he tried. Tanya saw that. He *wanted* to get it right. But soon, he began to stumble. Then pull back. Then turn cold.

But Tanya didn't give up right away. She stayed patient. She explained. She gave him space. She offered grace. Because to her, love wasn't just about receiving—it was about *building*. About teaching someone how to love you *right*. Even if it meant teaching him how to stay.

Life was better and brighter until Stylist was arrested. What followed were court dates, the ankle monitors, and whispered shame.

Tanya didn't flinch.

She stood by Stylist's side, no matter how deep the trouble ran. She answered every collect call without hesitation. She put money on his books.

She let his mother and brother move into her home when Stylist got locked up—her home, where her own four children were already stacked like bricks on her shoulders.

She fed them. Sheltered them. Extended kindness not because it was earned, but because it was *hers* to give.

But his mother wasn't easy. She made comments—shady ones, sharp enough to slice pride.

"She's too old for you," she poured the venom into Stylist's ears, loud enough for Tanya to hear. "Got all them kids… she gon' take everything you got."

Tanya heard it. Felt it. But she didn't snap.

She bit her tongue—not because she was weak, but because she had matured into a woman who knew that someone else's ignorance wasn't worth her peace. Still, it hurt. Because she had gone out of her way to make that woman feel like family, and family shouldn't turn their back when you're carrying everyone on yours.

Still, she stayed.

She stayed when Stylist had nothing to offer but a cluttered mind and a record heavy with mistakes. She stayed when he was juggling courtrooms, child support cases, and the fragile climb toward stability.

She stayed through funerals and holidays. Through heartbreak and hard times. She raised her children while holding him down with the kind of loyalty most people only *claim* to have.

She didn't stay because he was perfect. She stayed because she saw *potential*. Because she could see the man inside the mess. And she believed in *him.*

She never judged his past. Not even when his three children by different mothers brought drama to her doorstep did she support his relationships with them. Encouraged healing. Prayed for peace that wasn't even hers to pray for.

Because that's the kind of love Tanya gave—rare, raw, and unconditional, the kind that didn't just stick around for the good days, but showed up *especially* on the bad ones.

Tanya wasn't some woman chasing a fantasy. She had lived too much, seen too much, endured more than most— so she knew: real love is messy. It's layered. It's flawed. And it's never wrapped in perfection.

She wasn't in love with the money, the dates, or the flash. That was surface-level, temporary.

What held her was deeper. She was in love with Stylist—the boy who walked into her life with charm, chaos, and a broken story… and who slowly, under her patience, her faith, and her fire, began to become a man.

She saw past his mess. Past the noise. Past what his mother said, what the streets assumed, and what her friends whispered.

Because Tanya knew exactly who she was, and her worth was never up for debate.

Loving someone through their storms?

That wasn't a weakness.

That was power.

Because Tanya wasn't just some woman hoping to be chosen, she was the storm and the calm. The woman who prayed… and then became the answer.

Not just for herself, but for a man still learning what love really means.

8. From Setback to Soulwork

If there are no ups and downs, is life even life-ing? The struggle and the joy — they're both part of the ride.

Life was going pretty smoothly—until Stylist brought up something that made Tanya's heart tighten: he wanted a baby.

Tanya had heard it before. Sweetly at first. Then persistently. But her answer never changed. "I've been raising kids since I was a kid. I can't start over."

She thought of Ebony—what a great dad he was—present and loving to the children when they were together. But how disconnected he had been from their children after the breakup. How emotionally unavailable he remained.

She remembered the long nights filled with fevers, homework, and teenage arguments. She thought of her body, her freedom, her dreams.

And most of all, she thought of becoming someone's *fourth* baby's mama. She had sacrificed too much to let that become her label again.

So she held firm—even when the conversations got tense, even when Stylist looked disappointed.

***

Tanya had been working at Saint Cabrini Home for more than 20 years. It was the only job she had ever truly known—the place where she'd grown from a young mother into a woman who carried other people's pain and still smiled through her own.

But 2012 happened. And then, like a rug ripped from under her feet, the letter came: "The facility will be closing in 30 days. There will be no severance, no 401(k), no benefits. We are bankrupt."

Tanya sat in her car—clueless.

She had worked faithfully at Saint Cabrini Home for over two decades—giving her heart to children who weren't hers, finding purpose in service even when it exhausted her. But everything changed. The doors of Saint Cabrini closed for good.

There was utter silence and a void where her career used to live. She felt betrayed. She didn't know who she was without the job. She—for the first time in decades—had no plan.

At that time, Stylist was a big support. He didn't let her sit in that confusion too long.

"Why don't you start something for you?" he asked one night as they sat in silence. "You're always fixing everybody else. What if this is the sign to start building your own dream?"

At first, Tanya brushed it off. Shrugged. Smiled like the idea was too big to hold. But the thought lingered.

The betrayal had cut deep—not just emotionally, but financially. She had poured everything into that job, believing it would carry her to retirement. Instead, she found herself standing at a crossroads. And in that moment of uncertainty, she made a vow to herself:

Never again.

Never again would she be that dependent.

Never again would she let someone else hold the key to her future.

So, she did what Tanya had always done.

She bet on herself.

And soon, that was initially just a thought, turned into a vision—

Six months later, in the year 2012, in the heart of Poughkeepsie, *Hotties Boutique* was born.

With vision and fire, she opened her first women's boutique—a bold, unapologetic space. It was more than a business. It was a declaration.

It wasn't just a store. It was a movement. A message. ***"Everything Woman."*** That was her motto. Her mission. A reminder that she didn't just survive—she became.

The boutique sold non-surgical garments that shaped and molded bodies without a single needle. It was for every woman—big, small, young, old. Every woman who wanted to feel good without going under the knife. Every woman who had ever been told she wasn't enough.

Stylist was with her every step of the way. He helped fund it. Painted the walls. Installed the shelves. Passed out flyers on street corners and at hair salons. He braced and believed in Tanya in a way no one else ever had.

He helped scout locations. Paid contractors to fix the place up. Ordered her first rounds of inventory. Made sure the security shutter was up, and the space was warm and ready when she came from work. He didn't just support her dream—he helped build it.

And it flourished. The business ran successfully and brilliantly.

By day, Tanya worked at Kiddie Academy, opening the daycare center in the early morning hours. By afternoon, she opened up the doors to Hotties Boutique, welcoming women from all walks of life into a space that celebrated them.

Women came from across the different counties just to experience the energy inside Hotties Boutique. It wasn't just the products—it was Tanya's presence. Her story. Her strength. Her spirit.

She wasn't just selling shapewear. She was restoring confidence, one woman at a time.

***

Soon, Tanya and Stylist were celebrating their new home!

Before that, they had lived in a few different apartments together, working as a team and sharing household responsibilities.

Now they moved into their first home together, and things felt almost surreal. The girl who once cried herself to sleep in a broken apartment now had a backyard, a new kitchen, and peace.

It wasn't just a house—it was a symbol of growth, of struggle transformed into stability.

Blending their families was far from easy. Her four kids had their routines, their moods, their moments. Stylist had three of his own, navigating the awkwardness of weekend visits and co-parenting tension.

But somehow, they made it work. With time. With patience. With grace. Life wasn't all rainbows and cupcakes, but it wasn't all bitterness and hardships either.

To rejoice in their new place, to celebrate their new home, to cherish their good life, to revel in their success, Stylist surprised Tanya with a tiny teacup poodle—a sweet, wide-eyed pup with a pink bow and a personality as big as Stylist's love for her.

"She's for you," he said, grinning. "Something little to love that doesn't talk back."

They named her Nyla, and the bond was instant. Tanya, who had spent her life mothering everyone, finally had someone to spoil who didn't need discipline—just affection.

Nyla curled up at her feet while she worked, slept beside her at night, and followed her from room to room like a shadow of softness in a sometimes hard world.

58

Part III: Collapse

9. Tanya Unleashed

By 2013, Hotties Boutique had become more than a business—it was a *movement*. A name spoken with admiration in salons, whispered about in beauty supply aisles, and boldly tagged in Facebook groups from Newburgh to Albany. Word of mouth carried Tanya's vision across the Hudson Valley and beyond, faster than any paid ad could.

Women showed up not just for the products, but for her. Her warmth. Her honesty. Her energy. Tanya had that rare ability to make every customer feel seen. Whether it was a bride nervously shopping for shapewear under a tight wedding gown or a new mom searching for the confidence to love her postpartum body again, Tanya delivered.

She didn't just sell garments—she sold *transformation*.

And she was relentless with her marketing hustle. She took out bold, sassy ads in the Poughkeepsie Journal, each one stamped with her signature tagline: **"Everything Woman."**

She flooded Craigslist when it was still alive with random traffic, knowing some of her best customers might be scrolling late at night, looking for something, *anything* to make them feel whole again. She even created loyalty cards, handed out flyers at nail salons and daycares, and worked every angle of local marketing like it was gospel.

Her hustle was unmatched. And women felt that. They came in droves—not just for the shapewear, but for the spirit behind it.

Tanya was redefining beauty in a world that too often tried to shrink women down. And in the middle of that small city in New York, she was building something unforgettable—with faith, grit, and a whole lot of style.

***

It was there—inside the four pink walls of Hotties Boutique, between racks of corsets and body shapers—that Tanya met a man who would shift her world in the most unexpected way.

The email subject line read: *"Boutique Inquiry."* Short. Formal. Forgettable—until it wasn't.

They exchanged a few polite messages. He said he was interested in the boutique, but had "a unique request." Curious, Tanya agreed to a private appointment.

He arrived on a Thursday afternoon, buttoned up in a pressed shirt, khakis, and expensive leather shoes—but stood no taller than 5'5"—a short, slightly awkward Caucasian man, with soft eyes and nervous energy.

They sat alone in the boutique, the soft buzz of a playlist humming in the background. Small talk. A few awkward chuckles. Then he leaned in and said it: "I'm looking for someone to dominate me. Someone powerful. Beautiful. Assertive. Do you know anyone?"

Tanya blinked.

Confused. Intrigued. And just a little tickled.

He went on to explain—he ran a company, managed dozens of people, and made high-pressure decisions all day long. What he craved… was the opposite. To surrender. To be told what to do. To be controlled.

"No sex. No touching. Just domination," he said. "I'll pay anything. One hour."

Tanya's razor-sharp curiosity kicked in. The entrepreneur in her woke all the way up. She asked questions—boundaries, rules, expectations. She wanted to understand the psychology, not just for him, but for herself.

That night, she brought it up to Stylist. He was half-distracted, counting cash and handling side business—but he listened. His first instinct was skepticism. Then protection. Then… opportunity.

"As long as I'm there," Stylist said. "I need to make sure you're safe."

So they set the appointment. Stylist stayed close—just one room over. Calm. Alert. Watching over her.

Tanya stepped into character… Leather boots. Black lipstick. A cold stare and a commanding tone. And for one hour, she didn't raise her voice or a hand. She just… owned the room. And walked out $1,000 richer.

That night, sipping wine on their couch, she turned to Stylist and said: "This might be a thing." And it was.

Over the next few years, Tanya built a second lane of business quietly and privately. It wasn't something she advertised, and it didn't need neon lights. Word traveled through whispers, referrals, and discreet conversations.

What she created was more than a side hustle—it was a sanctuary for women who needed income without shame. She brought in women from all walks of life.

Some were young and curious, dipping a toe into the world of soft domination and power exchange. Some were older and refined, carrying wisdom, presence, and a calm kind of command.

Others were mothers, divorcees, nurses, or women just trying to make ends meet in a world that rarely made room for them.

Tanya trained them. Protected them. Paid them well.

She helped with bills, car notes, and rent, never taking more than she needed, and always giving more than expected.

No exploitation. No predators. Just an opportunity, with dignity attached.

The women ranged in age from 25 to 50, and they loved her for it. Because Tanya didn't judge, she didn't use. She guided. She became a protector. A teacher. A big sister. A boss. A blueprint.

And the clients?

High-level. Quiet. Powerful.

Judges. Surgeons. CEOs. Men who spent their lives being in control, but needed a space to surrender without consequence.

They came to Tanya's circle for something they couldn't get anywhere else: *Powerless moments in the presence of powerful women.*

And they paid well to keep it all silent.

Tanya wasn't just running a boutique anymore. She was running a movement behind closed doors—with elegance, with intention, and with control.

In the middle of all this thriving, Stylist ended up in prison for one year. No warning. No time to brace. Just a knock at the door, a court date, and a sentence that changed everything.

Before he left, he sat Tanya down. He handed her a stack of names, numbers, and handwritten instructions—contacts, suppliers, who to trust, who to avoid, how to keep his business breathing while he was gone.

And Tanya? She didn't wince or hesitate. She simply nodded, took the paper, and said, "I got it." Because that's who Tanya was—a woman who didn't fold under pressure.

While Stylist sat behind bars, Tanya ran everything. She juggled the whole kit and caboodle. She didn't just hold it down—she leveled it up. For him. For her. For everything they'd built.

But something changed in Tanya while Stylist was away.

Without a man constantly in her ear, without kids needing every minute of her attention, she felt free, for the first time in decades.

Her daughters were off at college. Her sons were grown, living with their girlfriends. Tamel had a daughter now. And Dazjohn had three sons of his own.

She was a grandmother four times over—and still bad.

She went out. She drank. She danced. She laughed out loud and came home late.

Money was plentiful.

Her boutique was booming by day, and her alternative business? Thriving by night.

She rubbed shoulders with women she never would've met in her old life—CEOs, nurses, strippers, magicians, accountants, social workers, real estate agents. Women with degrees and women with grit. Women with war stories and wild dreams. And they all found something in Tanya—confidence, comfort, or a safe place to be raw.

She became more than a boutique owner. She became a network. A whispered name in the right circles. A woman who saw other women and helped them rise.

She started frequenting strip clubs—not to chase anything, but to study. To connect. To listen.

And that's where she made a deep connection with the club owner—a quiet, calculating businessman who respected her hustle. It didn't take long before Tanya stepped into a new role: *House Mother*.

No, she wasn't on stage. She was backstage. In the dressing rooms. In the heart of it.

She provided everything from lashes to lingerie, Band-Aids to baby wipes, pep talks to protection plans.

To the dancers, Tanya became part mentor, part auntie, part fixer. She saw them—not as broken or reckless—but as businesswomen, as survivors, as sisters.

And she never did it alone. Her best friend Aja was right there beside her—sorting outfits, helping the girls get dressed, picking out what looked best, making sure every detail was handled.

Aja came with her own set of life lessons, her own fire, but her loyalty never wavered. Whatever Tanya needed, Aja delivered. Always. She was a true ride-or-die—the kind of woman you could call at midnight, and she'd show up, no questions asked.

Though Aja was eventually married and settled down, followed by a pregnancy, and wasn't as available as before, still, whether it was crying over lost love, packing inventory at the boutique, or driving through the city at midnight just to clear their heads, they did it together.

And the club?

It wasn't just nightlife. It became a new branch of her empire.

Tanya had evolved not just into a boss but into a woman completely in charge of her own story. By this point in her life, Tanya wasn't surviving anymore—she was thriving.

She was bold, brilliant, and flatteringly in her element. Not boxed in by motherhood. Not chained to a man. Not limited by what society said, a woman with four grown kids and four grandkids could do.

She was living out loud, unapologetically. Her life was a collage of glamour, grit, and growth.

From grief to power.

From pain to purpose.

And she wasn't done yet. This was just the next chapter, and Tanya was writing it her way. And in this chapter of her life, Tanya didn't just have money, businesses, or beauty— she had balance. She had peace. She had true sisterhood.

After years of living in survival mode, Tanya was finally beginning to live in her own skin. No longer just someone's mother, someone's woman, or someone's lifeline—she was rediscovering herself.

Slowly. Intentionally. Powerfully.

With Hotties Boutique still buzzing and a quiet peace settling into her life, she found herself reconnecting with an old teenage friend, Tasha.

They had shared laughs, secrets, and teen dreams back in the day. Now, decades later, they were sharing life for a second time—grown woman style. Tasha was a hairdresser who did Tanya's hair, and that's how they reconnected and started hanging out again.

Every morning, they hit the gym—sweating out stress, past pain, and everything that once weighed them down- and after workouts came coffee. Sometimes, matinee movies. Sometimes, late-night dancing like they were youngsters again.

Tasha became her mirror, her diary. She brought a breath of fresh air to a world that could still feel heavy. With Tasha, Tanya didn't have to explain her strength—or apologize for her softness. They had seen each other grow, fall, rise, and glow.

She didn't judge. She didn't flinch. She was lungful when the world suffocated her. Advice when life got confusing. And laughter when things got dark.

10.   Tanya & The Bats

Tanya was living a fulfilling life when something distinctive happened. She started to receive signs from the unseen.

Before that, Stylist had just come home from his year-long prison bid. He walked through the door with excitement in his eyes and promises on his lips—talk of rebuilding, of doing right, of picking up where they left off.

Tanya welcomed him. His presence still warmed her. But something was… off. The scent of old habits clung to him like cheap cologne. At first, it was just a drink or two.

Then it became bottles. Then pills. Then the parties. Loud music. New faces. Strange energy. Nights that started late and ended with regret.

His eyes weren't as clear as his words. And the man she held down while he was locked away… was slipping through her fingers.

Still, Tanya kept her head and heart grounded. She didn't fall apart—she stayed focused.

Meanwhile, Tanya's daughters stepped up, helping out at Hotties Boutique when they were home from college.

They brought laughter, new music, and a glow that the customers adored. They were reflections of her—bright, driven, unstoppable.

Dazjohn, her youngest, was now living in New Jersey, building his own family, making Tanya a grandmother once again. She smiled at his growth.

But then came the call no mother wants: Tamel, her oldest, had been picked up—a loaded gun charge. Just like that, he was gone.

It rocked her not just because he was her son. But because he was the first. The one who watched her struggle and rise—the one who grew up too fast because she had to survive.

Tanya felt the weight deep in her bones. But she didn't let it break her. She let it refine her. Because that's what life kept teaching her: Pressure makes diamonds. Pain shapes power. And love—when it's real—survives even the darkest storms.

Tanya's test wasn't over. Not long after, on a rainy Wednesday morning, the phone rang. Tanya had just finished steaming garments for a new window display at Hotties Boutique.

She was prepping for the weekend rush—her shop had become the go-to spot for women looking to transform their bodies and reclaim their confidence.

But none of that mattered when she heard the voice on the other end. "Ma… they got me."

It was Dazjohn, her youngest.

Her stomach dropped. She already knew. She didn't need the details. She just needed to sit down.

Sale of a controlled substance. That's what they said.

Just like that, both of her sons were behind bars.

Her mind raced. *Not Dazjohn, too. Not her baby—the one with the big laugh, the big heart. The second in command. The one who used to sneak extra snacks into his backpack to sell to the kids at school who didn't have any.*

She dropped the phone and sat in silence. "Ya Allah," she whispered, tears pooling in her eyes. "What am I doing wrong? What did I miss?"

Tanya prided herself on being strong. A woman who rose from trauma and poverty. A woman who fought to give her children better than what she had. And now?

Tamel, her oldest, was in prison on a gun charge.

Dazjohn, her youngest, had just been taken in.

Her two daughters were away at college, thriving.

And she was here—heart full, hands tied.

The guilt was unbearable. She didn't cry in front of people. But that night, with Stylist asleep and the house quiet, she sat on the edge of the bed, grabbed her prayer mat, and wept into sujood.

"Allah, I tried. I tried to be a good mother. I tried to show them the right. Why them? Why my boys?"

There were no answers—only the stillness of the room and the low hum of the streetlights outside.

Tanya held them down.

Every week, she wrote letters. Not just "stay strong" or "I love you," but real letters—reminders of who they were, affirmations of who they could still become.

She sent money for commissary, food packages, birthday cards, and books. She kept their photos on her boutique desk. She made sure no one forgot their names.

Still, the ache lingered.

She missed seeing their faces. Missed calling them on the phone or FaceTiming to hear their voices. Missed traveling down to Jersey to see Coop and his two boys.

Missed being a mom in motion instead of a mom in mourning.

She'd walk into an empty room and sit in the dark.

Stylist tried to be supportive, but he didn't always understand. He was still living by his own code—hustling, partying, trapped in cycles that Tanya was slowly outgrowing.

Their love remained, but their paths were beginning to diverge. The house was quieter now.

She'd hear laughter from her daughters on the phone—stories about college life, new friends, big dreams. That brought her joy. But at night, when the laughter faded and the boutique closed, she felt the weight of her boys' absence like bricks on her chest.

She wondered if she had failed them. If there was something she could've done differently. If the streets pulled stronger than her prayers.

But she didn't give up. Tanya wore her grief like armor. She showed up every day at the boutique with a smile for her clients—makeup flawless, energy high.

No one saw the heaviness she carried behind those lashes. No one saw how often she prayed in the backroom between fittings.

Her boys were locked away, but she made sure their names stayed alive. She encouraged them to study, to write, to build something inside. She reminded them, again and again, that their story wasn't over.

Because a mother doesn't stop loving just because the world tries to write her children off.

She told her sons, Tamel & Dazjohn, in a letter: *"This isn't who you are. This is just where you are. But where you are today doesn't have to be where you stay. I'm still proud of you. Even now. Especially now."*

She kept every letter they wrote back. Sometimes, she'd reread them with tears. Sometimes with laughter. And even though she often felt helpless, she reminded herself that presence was power, and she was present. For them. Always.

***

While Tanya felt a mother's weight, she missed her own mom. Remembered her in all the ways she could—the strength behind the struggle.

Growing up, Tanya always knew her mother was strong. She didn't understand the full extent of her mother's battles—she just knew there was always food on the table, clothes in the closet, and love in the home.

Her mother was loud, funny, stylish, and present. She'd show up to school functions with a big smile, cheering louder than anyone else in the room.

To the outside world, it looked like they had it all together. But beneath the surface, her mother carried a heavy secret: She was struggling with drug addiction.

As a child, Tanya didn't see the signs. She chalked up the mood swings to stress. She thought the long absences were just part of grown-up life.

Her mother hid the truth well, functioning, providing, and protecting her children with everything she had, even while she was barely holding herself together.

Some nights, Tanya would hear her mother crying through the walls. She never knew why. And when the crying stopped, she simply assumed things had gotten better.

It wasn't until years later—when Tanya enrolled in a CASAC program (Credentialed Alcoholism and Substance Abuse Counselor)—that the pieces began to fall into place.

She studied the cycles. The behaviors. The pain behind the disease. And suddenly, her childhood made sense in a new, painful, and powerful way.

It was heartbreaking to realize her mother had been suffering in silence. But it was also healing as she finally understood: addiction wasn't weakness. It was a disease.

And her mother had been fighting it every single day— while showing up, feeding them, loving them, and holding the household together.

Later, in 2022, something miraculous happened. Her mother got clean. After years of silent struggle, she made the brave decision to stop using. She's been clean and sober ever since.

Now, she shows up for her children and grandchildren not just physically—but emotionally, spiritually, fully. She's active in their lives. Encouraging. Present. Loving in ways only a healed mother can be.

Tanya is so proud of her.

She remembers all the nights she prayed—whispering into the dark, begging God to bring her mother out of that place. When the day came, it felt like the sun finally broke through years of clouds.

She sees her mother now for who she truly is: A woman who never gave up. Not on herself. Not on her family.

Her journey is one of quiet courage and incredible redemption. She herself—now a woman who has learned to understand pain instead of merely surviving it—carries that same strength with her everywhere she goes.

***

Stylist and Tanya had shifted into their new home. They had bought it together—a beautiful but aging home with secrets of its own.

Back home, Tanya found herself spending more time in the house. *It* started subtly, with a flutter. Then a squeak.

Then… bats.

At first, she panicked, grabbed a broom, and opened every window in a frenzy. But it kept happening. And something about the timing—the patterns, the frequency— made her pause.

They always came between 2 and 3 in the morning. Two to three times a month. This didn't feel random. These didn't feel like pests. They felt like messengers.

She began to read about them. It turned out that bats symbolize rebirth. Intuition. Letting go of the past and thriving in darkness.

Tanya—alone in the stillness of that house—couldn't help but wonder: Maybe they weren't invading. Maybe they were guiding.

Perhaps it wasn't just about the bats. It was about her. She was shedding old skins. Old versions of herself. Letting go of the woman who always carried, fixed, and forgave. She was no longer in survival mode. She was in alignment.

One night, Tanya sat quietly in her bedroom and whispered, "Allah, are You trying to tell me something?"

The bats had become a symbol—a divine nudge.

She started playing the local numbers, chasing the feeling that her luck was shifting. Each time a bat appeared, she bought a Powerball quick pick.

But soon, it became about more than money. Tanya began to wonder if Allah wanted something profounder from her. Wanted her to slow down. To release the drinking. The late nights. The dominatrix hustle had once brought fast cash, but cost her small pieces of her soul each time.

One afternoon over coffee, she shared it all with Tasha. Tasha leaned back, raised a brow, and said, "Girl… bats are spiritual. That's your ancestors. Your spirit guides. Maybe even God Himself is trying to wake you up." Tanya took that to heart. But change didn't happen overnight.

Though Stylist was still around, the energy between them had shifted. She was no longer the same woman who waited on him. She no longer moved around his rhythm—

She moved in alignment with her own. She had evolved—crafted her own rhythm, her own world. Yes, she still indulged from time to time—a drink here, a night out there. But even her fun felt different now.

Her mind was clearer. Her spirit was reaching for something higher. She started letting go of old patterns, one by one. Stylist noticed the change, but couldn't quite grasp it. He was chasing the past. She was chasing purpose.

Through it all, Tanya leaned on what held her: Stylist— always attentive, always there, quietly loving her; her mom and stepdad, who never hesitated to help, even removing bats from the house; her children; her boutique; her friends, Raquel, Ann, and Tasha; and her unwavering faith. Each piece of her world gave her strength, and none could be left out.

The bats kept coming. So did the dreams. So did the clarity. Tanya was being called to transform—again. A road trip. The plan was simple: Tanya and her daughters would pack up the car and take a road trip to North Carolina to visit their aunt and grandfather—their dad's side of the family.

Though she and Ebony had long gone their separate ways, Tanya still considered his people her own. They were family, too.

The three of them were supposed to hit the road—just the girls—windows down, music loud, hearts open. The conversations were meant to be healing. A chance to laugh until their stomachs hurt, to talk about life, love, and everything in between.

Tanya longed to feel like herself again. To feel free. The open road was meant to be a reminder: She still had living to do. She still had dreams of her own. And she wanted her girls to see that. To know that joy was still possible, even after heartbreak. That healing could be found in motion, in miles, in memories made together.

11.　　The Day the Sky Fell

It was a hot and humid June of 2018 in Poughkeepsie, NY, and something unthinkable happened. The warm midsummer day started unhurriedly. Clouds rolled in softly and slowly like whispers of change.

It was supposed to be a normal day—a regular Thursday. But fate had a different plan. In a blink, it all came crashing down—literally.

The sky was calm that morning, but inside Tanya was a storm she didn't see coming. One moment, she was standing on solid ground, and the next, everything gave way.

She could still hear the sound of the walls crumbling— the sharpness of screams echoing through thick dust and chaos. Under the rubble, time stood still. But even as pain surged through her body, something within whispered, *You are not done*. That whisper became the heartbeat of her survival.

***

Tanya sat on the edge of her bed, twisting the gold ring on her finger as she talked to Tasha on the phone. They hadn't seen each other in a couple of weeks, and both were itching for some girl time.

"Let's do lunch," Tanya said.

"I'm off at three. I'll swing by after work."

Stylist was in the next room, scrolling through his phone, half-listening to a podcast. Tanya peeked around the corner.

"Babe, can you head to the boutique and open the shutters for me before I get there later? I don't feel like wrestling with them again."

He nodded without looking up. "I got you."

Tanya left for her shift at Dutchess County BOCES, her last week before summer break. The school year was winding down, and spirits were light. The staff meeting that morning was brief—scheduled for an hour but done in fifteen minutes. Tanya smiled. That meant more time to prep at Hotties Boutique, her sanctuary.

Before heading towards the boutique, Tanya went down to Downstate Correctional Facility to visit her son, Dazjohn. The visit was warm and welcoming. They talked about current events, updates on the family, her plans for the summer now that school was out, and how he had been feeling. After spending that time together, she said her goodbyes and left.

She was supposed to meet Tasha for lunch. The plan was to rendezvous at the boutique once Tanya left the correctional facility.

She arrived at her shop like she always did—arms full of new merchandise and her heart full of purpose. The boutique smelled like Fabuloso and fresh possibilities. The pink walls were bright and welcoming, lined with waist trainers, sleek mannequins, and rhinestone accents. The boutique was her baby. Her second chance. Her resurrection.

She unpacked a few items, hung up a new shipment, and sat behind the register in the corner with her iced coffee. She settled in and waited for Tasha so they could head out and enjoy their lunch together.

While she was sipping on her coffee and waiting for her friend, she grabbed her phone and dialed DSW to check on the status of a pair of shoes she had ordered for the upcoming road trip with her daughters to North Carolina.

"Thank you for calling DSW. How may I help you?"

"Hi, my name is Tanya. I'm calling about an order I placed…"

Suddenly, the sky darkened. A cold gust of wind whipped past the window. Then came the rain—heavy and erratic, pelting against the boutique's glass like it was angry. A quick flash of lightning filled the room with white light.

The DSW rep's voice was still on the line. "Please hold while I check the status of your order…"

And then—BOOM. A deafening explosion shook the air. Her phone flew from her hand. Black smoke, splintered wood, sheetrock, and shattered glass filled every inch of the boutique. The scent of burned rubber and chemicals overwhelmed her senses.

Debris pinned her legs. A heavy piece of sheetrock cracked against her forehead. Everything slowed down. She blinked, blood dripping down her face. She reached up, confused, disoriented, and then froze.

She could see outside through the hole in the roof. "What the hell happened?" All around her were the remnants of her dream—destroyed in an instant.

She looked to her right and saw a photo of Stylist, still hanging on the wall, somehow untouched. Below it, a framed picture of her sons—Tamel and Dazjohn. The edges were blackened with soot, but the image remained.

She tried to move, but pain surged through her arm. A nail had torn through her skin. She pulled her hand back and felt hot blood trickle down her sleeve.

"Am I dreaming? Is this real?"

Then she heard it faintly— "Hello? Hello? Are you there?" The DSW rep's voice, distant and panicked, still crackled through the phone.

Tanya stared at the phone just out of reach, her hand pinned beneath rubble. She didn't cry. She didn't scream. She just… sat still.

An explosion. Thunder. Screams. And then silence, broken only by the shifting groans of the broken building settling into itself like a wounded beast.

Tanya had been buried alive. She didn't know exactly how long she'd been trapped. She only knew the darkness was absolute.

For a moment, she accepted it. Accepted that this might be it. Accepted that maybe this was how she would leave the world—buried beneath the ashes of something she built from scratch.

"You have life insurance. Your kids will be okay," she thought. "You've always had it. Ever since Saint Cabrini Home. You prepared."

Her mind wandered to Tamel and Dazjohn, in prison, to her daughters, who were blossoming in college. She thought of how hard she tried, how much she gave, how much she loved.

And then a voice—her own voice—rose from deep within. "Call out. Somebody will hear you."

But Tanya hesitated. Because deep down, she didn't believe anyone would care enough to come. Not the police. Not the fire department. Not even Stylist. She felt invisible, unworthy of being rescued.

But her subconscious wouldn't let her go. "Yell, Tanya. Yell. TRY."

So she did. Weakly at first. Then louder. "HELLO? HELLO? IS ANYBODY OUT THERE? HELP ME!" She repeated it. Again. And again.

"HELP! HELP! PLEASE!" She screamed until her throat was raw, hoping someone—anyone—would hear her. And finally, through the silence, came a voice.

"I think that lady's in there!"

Then the most beautiful sound: fire engine sirens, cutting through the chaos like a promise. Relief washed over her—not fear, not panic, but calm. Someone was coming.

She heard something… voices outside… sirens in the distance… the muffled thud of footsteps running. Help was coming. Not because she believed she was worthy. But because she chose to fight for herself anyway.

The firefighters arrived quickly, assessing the damage. What they didn't realize was that they were standing on top of her; the very ground beneath their boots was Tanya's prison.

When they finally located her under the wreckage, they radioed in for a trauma doctor. Her left leg was so pinned that the only plan was amputation.

Upon the arrival of a doctor and when he crawled into the debris, face covered in sweat and soot, and saw her—talking, directing, alert, sharp—he stopped.

"She's too present. Too alive," he said. "We're not cutting that leg off. Not like this. Find another way."

But time was slipping. Another storm was fast approaching. The fire chief came in, stern and commanding. "If we can't get her out in 15 minutes, we pull out. I'm not risking any more lives."

Tanya heard every word. And something inside her broke. "YOU DON'T CARE ABOUT ME!" she shouted. "IF I WERE WHITE, YOU WOULDN'T LEAVE ME HERE! BECAUSE I'M BLACK, YOU'RE GIVING UP!"

Her voice echoed through the broken boutique. The firefighters paused, shaken.

Anyhow, fifteen minutes passed. The storm was nearing. The fire chief came on the radio. "Pull out. Everyone. Now."

The team began retreating, reluctantly. But one firefighter, a young man with kind eyes and a haunted expression, turned back. "Lady, I swear to you—I'll be back. We have to regroup. The plan's not working, but we're not leaving you." He began to walk away.

"Yo, firefighter!" Tanya called. "Can you hand me that wig over there?"

He turned, confused. "That wig? It's no good. It's got nails in it, soot. It's ruined."

"I can't be on camera like this. Y'all got cameras, drones… People watching. I can't be seen looking like this."

He smiled, despite the pain of the moment, and handed her the wig.

Tanya took one look and sighed. "You're right… I can't wear this. It's a mess."

"Told you. But you're beautiful and brave as it is…" he said gently, walking off. "I'll be back."

Scenes from the building collapse on Academy Street in the City of Poughkeepsie on June 18, 2018.

The top of 19 Academy St. in the City of Poughkeepsie collapsed Monday, dropping debris and causing damage at other properties.

Tanya was alone again. Hours had passed. She didn't know how long anymore. Her feet were numb. Her legs throbbed with pain. She was bleeding and fading fast. But she wasn't giving up.

As the weight of the rubble crushed her body, Tanya felt herself slipping—slipping away from pain, slipping away from sound, slipping away from life. The screams, the sirens, the frantic voices of firefighters blurred into silence.

With shaking arms, she started moving pieces of wood. Pipes. Nails. Slowly. Desperately. She managed to free her right foot and lift it onto a nearby desk.

She turned to work on the left. That's when her world began to tilt. Dizzy. Weak. Cold. She was losing blood. Fading. Her hands slithered. Her breath slowed. And then… silence.

She didn't wake up. Not right away. She found herself in a strange space. And then—nothing. No light. No tunnel. Just blackness.

It wasn't darkness like nightfall. It was deeper. Endless. Infinite. Like floating in outer space with no stars, no planets, no time. Just vast, quiet black.

Tanya didn't see her life flash before her eyes. She didn't see angels or ancestors. She didn't feel fear or panic. Instead, she felt something else—something unexplainable. A presence. Not a face, not a voice, but a force that wrapped around her like invisible arms. It was heavy and weightless all at once. Still and vast. Familiar, but foreign.

"I don't wanna be here," she whispered—or thought—she wasn't sure. Her voice didn't echo, but the words felt heard. "Please send me back. I don't wanna be here."

She didn't beg out of fear. She wasn't afraid of what was happening. But she knew she wasn't done. Not yet. Not like this. Somewhere deep inside her spirit, a fire lit. Her children, her dreams, her unfinished purpose—all surged up through her soul like a silent scream.

And then, in a blink, breath returned. The weight of her chest. The burning pain in her limbs. The cold air of reality rushed in. She came back—to rubble, to rescue, to survival.

A few moments later—light. There was movement. Hands. Tanya opened her eyes to bright lights and loud voices. She was on a stretcher, being lifted into an ambulance.

She had been buried for six lengthy hours. But she survived. Broken but not beaten. Covered in dust and blood, but very much alive.

But Tanya's not gonna ever forget this place. The moment between life and whatever comes next. It wasn't heaven, it wasn't hell. It was something more mysterious. A holding place. A divine pause. And in that pause, she chose to fight.

Tanya's car, after the incident

12.　　Call to The Loved Ones

Ebony *(spoken softly, shakily)*:

I was just getting out of the shower… towel on my head, lotion half on. Conner was folding laundry as if it were just another Saturday.

Then my phone rang. I almost ignored it—but something told me to pick it up.

And when I did… my world stopped.

"Something happened to Ma."

That's all they said. No details. No comfort. Just those five words, hitting like a punch to the chest.

I dropped everything. I was shaking so bad that Conner had to grab my arm.

I kept asking, "What? What happened? What's going on?" But nobody had answers.

All I could think was—my mama… the strongest woman I know… is she gone? God, please no. Please don't take my mother.

***

Tamel *(with restrained emotion)*:

I was in my cell, reading—just another day behind these cold-ass walls. Then a CO came by and said, "You got a call. Family emergency."

My stomach dropped. Ain't nothing good come from those words.

When I heard Ebony's voice, my knees damn near gave out. She said, "Ma's hurt. It's bad."

I felt powerless. Like, how the hell am I supposed to protect my mother from in here?

She visited me. She prayed for me. She never gave up on me. And now she needed me—and I couldn't do a damn thing. Just stand there in a prison hallway and cry in silence.

***

Dazjohn *(angrily, voice cracking)*:

They called me off the yard. At first, I thought, "What now?" But when they said it was about Ma… man, I felt like my heart got ripped out of my chest.

She's my everything. My backbone. My peace when my mind's at war. She always said, *"Boy, when you come home, you're gonna shine."* But now I might come home to a world without her in it?

I turned away from everybody and cried. Hard. No shame in it. Because when you got a mama like ours, the thought of losing her—it'll break you down.

***

Emani *(quiet, breathless)*:

I was at work. Helping customers, smiling, being fake happy. Then my phone lit up—missed calls, texts, panic everywhere.

I ran to the break room and called back. Ebony answered. And her voice… She said, *"Ma's been in an accident. It's serious."*

I couldn't breathe. I literally felt the air leave my body. I kept saying, "No, no, no."

I don't even remember leaving work. I just knew I had to get to her. I had to see her with my own eyes. Because I couldn't lose my mother, I wouldn't.

***

Together *(softly, overlapping)*:

We didn't know how bad it was. We just knew our world wasn't right. We were scared… we were broken… we were lost without her.

Ebony *(tears in her voice)*: But even in that moment, I held on to one thing… my *faith*.

Tamel: My *prayers.*

Dazjohn: My *hope.*

Emani: Because if anybody could come back from the edge of death… It's our *mama*.

***

Mama Glo *(stuttering, gasping)*:

The phone rang, and it was my niece Chrissy, her voice shaking. 'Mama Glo,' she said, barely able to get the words out, 'the building collapsed—Tanya's Boutique is gone… and Tanya's in it.'

In that instant, the world tilted. My knees buckled as the weight of those words sank in, turning an ordinary day into the darkest moment of our lives.

Not my baby. Not Tanya.

I'm on my way!

I gripped the steering wheel so tightly that my knuckles turned white. My heart pounded in my ears, drowning out every sound except the echo of Chrissy's trembling words: *Tanya's in the building.*

My mind fought against it—refusing to believe, praying with every red light, every turn of the road. But when I arrived and saw the fire trucks, the crowd, and the smoke curling into the sky, my body went weak.

I stumbled forward, tears stinging my eyes, calling my daughter's name as if my voice alone could pull her from the rubble.

***

Stylist *(frantic, yelling):*

At King Street Park, my phone rang—it was Aja, frantic. "Stylist... Tanya's Boutique... It's gone. She's buried."

My breath caught. I'd just spoken to her. She had a meeting at BOCES. This couldn't be real.

Yet moments later, I was tearing through the streets toward the scene. When I arrived, someone said they'd seen her car parked behind the building. My stomach dropped. I pushed past the crowd, ignoring firefighters telling me to stay back.

Smoke burned my lungs as my eyes swept the wreckage. But I kept moving and shouting, I have to get to her. I have to get her out.

***

Ebony *(ex-husband):*

Even though Tanya and I were no longer together, I still stopped by the Boutique often—just to check on her, share a laugh, or grab a plate of food she'd fix for me and my young son.

So when the news hit that Tanya's Boutique had collapsed—and that she was buried inside—my heart seized. Shock gave way to urgency. I have to get over there.

My mind raced to my daughters, Ebony and Emani— where were they? Were they safe?

Pulling up to the scene, I wasn't just there to see what was happening; I was there to be a pillar for my children, to stand watch, to be present in the middle of a nightmare none of us could wake from.

13.   Beauty in Brutality

Tanya opened her eyes to the strobe-like flicker of red and white lights. The air was thick with the sterile scent of alcohol wipes, metal, and blood—her blood.

She couldn't move, couldn't speak, just feel. Every inch of her body screamed, but it was her feet—her foundation— that felt like they were no longer a part of her.

She was in an ambulance, oxygen mask strapped across her face, heart monitor beeping frantically. Her body was strapped down, but her mind was running wild.

"What happened to me?"

"Where are my babies?"

"Am I going to die?"

The paramedic, a young woman with freckles and panic in her eyes, looked down at Tanya and gave her a trembling smile. It was the kind of smile you give someone when you don't know if they'll make it.

"You're doing great, Tanya. Just hold on. We're almost there."

***

Saint Francis Hospital—its name glowed on the ER entrance like a tired promise. They wheeled her in, and she watched the ceiling tiles blur above her like an old film reel.

Nurses barked orders. "Someone cut off her shirt." A male nurse gasped when he pulled back the blanket and saw her feet. "My God… Her feet are gone."

Tanya couldn't look, but she could feel—not physically, the morphine was working on that—but spiritually, soul-deep. Her foundation—the very thing she used to walk into rooms with power, strut through life with purpose—had been shattered.

The very first thing that happened after she was rolled into the ER was a very young and handsome black doctor noticing the split in her forehead.

He started working on it, and Tanya told him to stitch it very small—she didn't want a big scar on her face. He nodded and worked with careful precision, and when he was done, it was perfect. He did an excellent job.

***

Outside, the hospital buzzed with urgency. Phones rang off the hook, notifications pinged nonstop: *"Is she okay?"* *"What happened?"* *"We're praying!"* The whole community came out to check on Tanya's status. Everyone was concerned. Her mom had even been admitted temporarily so she could stay close, right next to Tanya.

In the blur of sirens and flashing lights, Raquel rushed towards Tanya's daughters, who were turned crisis commanders. She didn't say a word at first—just wrapped them in a fierce, quivering hug, holding on as if she could keep them from falling apart.

Not far off, Ebony and Emani saw their father, standing near the police tape, a cigarette burning slowly in the rain. He didn't say much. Didn't have to. The girls looked him in the eyes, and he knew—he was needed now, really needed.

The girls ran up to him. They started hugging and crying, amid that, Ebony reminded them that he was there for them and that their mom would be totally OK.

Over to the side was Stylist… but he didn't feel any of that family reunion. He just wanted Tanya to be well. He was in that cold hospital hallway, alone in a building full of people: nobody but him and her.

The place was overloaded with people who wanted to reach out to Tanya. Security had to turn away additional visitors; the ER was at full capacity, and no more waiting-room seats were available.

Yet even from afar, everyone was there in spirit, holding space for her, holding her in their prayers. The community's love pressed in, palpable, as if their prayers could push through the walls and wrap Tanya in strength.

***

The first night was a blur and passed in fragments. Tanya drifted in and out of consciousness, her mind skipping like a scratched record—between memories of her boutique, her kids' faces, Stylist's crooked grin, and the sound of collapsing sheetrock.

By the second day, she was more alert. That's when the doctors came in—white coats, somber faces. And the weight of the bad news was hanging in the air.

The lead surgeon didn't waste time. "Tanya... you're a strong woman. You survived something most people don't. But your injuries... they're beyond what we can treat here."

He paused. She stared. The room seemed to shrink.

"Both of your feet sustained crush injuries. There's extensive damage—ligaments torn, bones shattered, multiple severed toes, and… there's a nail lodged through the top of your left foot. Your right foot is literally split in half, down the center."

Her stomach tightened.

"You'll need to be transferred to Westchester Medical Center. It's a trauma facility with a higher surgical capability."

Silence.

Tanya blinked. She nodded. Then she laughed. It wasn't joyful—it was that hollow, jagged laugh people give right before a scream tears its way out.

"So… you're telling me the girl with the pink walls and six-inch heels is gonna leave this hospital with no goddamn feet?"

The nurse gasped.

The doctor remained quiet.

Tanya stared at the ceiling.

She wanted to cry. But she couldn't. She wouldn't give them that. She was a mother, a warrior, a hustler, a lover, and a survivor.

Despite all the courage she managed to gather, in that moment, lying in a hospital bed with her legs bound in bandages and her sense of self unraveling, she felt like a young girl again—vulnerable, scared, alone.

She remembered being ten years old, falling off her bike, and ripping her knee open. She ran inside, crying, and her grandmother looked her dead in the eyes and said…

"Tanya, pain doesn't mean you're weak. Pain means you're alive. You bleeding? Good. That means you got something left to fight with."

Lying in that hospital bed now, she remembered those words like a prayer. Like prophecy. She was bleeding again. From the feet this time. But she was alive. And if she were alive, she could fight. And if she could fight… she could rebuild.

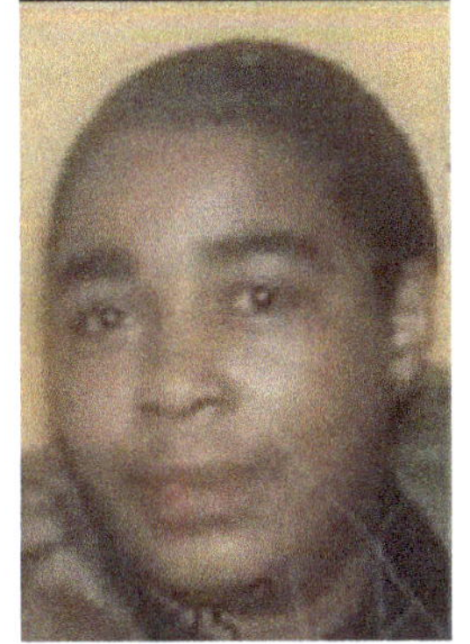

Tanya's grandmother, Dottie

This wasn't the end of Tanya. This was the start of something else. Something raw. Something real. Something unfuckwithable.

14.　　Still Standing

The ambulance siren howled through the Hudson Valley darkness, tearing the summer night wide open. Inside, Tanya lay strapped to a gurney, IV lines swaying with every bump in the road, her feet wrapped in thick gauze and trauma. Blood. Bone. Bandages. But never broken. Not Tanya.

Stylist followed close behind in his car, headlights cutting through the rain, until he reached Westchester Medical Center.

When the ambulance hit Westchester Medical Center, it was like rolling into a different dimension. The air was colder, cleaner. The halls were vast. The floors glowed.

This was the trauma center—the best in New York State—and they were ready. Tanya was wheeled in like royalty under siege. Her chart was a novella. Her injuries were a roadmap of hell.

The moment she was admitted, Stylist was there—never leaving her side. Beside her, Stylist sat stiff, silent. His hoodie was soaked in rain and sweat. His hands trembled, gripping the metal bar of the stretcher like it was the last real thing he could hold onto in this world. He didn't cry. He just stared at her—this woman, his woman—who had just been buried alive for six hours and still cracked jokes like she was at a backyard cookout.

Tanya turned her head toward him, her voice hoarse but firm: "Go home, Stylist. Shower. Eat. Rest."

Stylist shook his head. "Nah. I ain't going nowhere. I'm not leaving you. I can't leave you."

He meant it because, truth be told? Without Tanya, he was just air. Just smoke. Just echoes.

While Tanya was admitted to the hospital, her teacup poodle, Nyla, was given to Ebony by Stylist so she could take care of her.

Within the first 24 hours, Tanya was scheduled for seven surgeries.

Pins in her feet.

Skin grafts on her legs.

Debris removal from her lungs and heart.

Ligament reconstruction.

Tanya opened her eyes to white walls and machines humming like a lullaby she never asked for. Tubes were attached to places she couldn't feel. Her legs, wrapped and heavy, didn't move when she told them to.

But her spirit? That moved mountains. Each nurse who smiled, each prayer whispered over her, each hand that held hers, helped stitch the pieces of her back together. The hospital wasn't just where she healed physically—it became a sanctuary of transformation.

She should've been broken. But Tanya? She became a legend on the trauma floor. From trauma nurses to janitors, from cafeteria staff to night shift security guards—everyone knew her.

They brought her extra Jell-O and snuck in snacks. They asked to braid her hair. Sat and listened to her tell stories about her boutique, her kids, her dreams.

They allowed Tasha to put lashes on her and do her hair one day. They had the whole trauma floor smoking because she was getting her hair flat-ironed. Tasha brought her a 24-inch weave and busted it down bone straight right there next to her IV pole.

She had two of the best doctors in Westchester, Dr. Shaner and Dr. Zelner, who did a wonderful job on the surgeries to get her feet back together and clear the debris from her body.

The head nurse whispered, "You're the toughest thing I've seen come through these doors in years." And the trauma surgeon? He said he'd never seen someone still laughing through skin grafts.

Tanya said, "Listen, y'all ain't got no tequila or Newports here, so what the hell am I supposed to do?"

Her story was all over the news. It traveled like gospel.

The boutique owner was buried alive and survived six hours under rubble. Never lost her mind. Never lost her light—Tanya from the Pink Boutique.

Her friend from Africa even called: "Yo, I saw you on the news out here. Tanya, you made it to the motherland."

Her village showed the fuck up. Raquel, her sister/friend, made sure her bills were paid. She made sure that Tanya's daughters were OK and helped them with anything. They needed to support their mom, and her village showed out for her, bringing the vibes, keeping her laughing, smiling, and in a positive, upbeat mood.

Her mama sat next to her bed and prayed with oil on her fingers. Her daughters snuggled beside her on the hospital cot. Even the security guard asked if she wanted her boutique logo printed on her walker.

Stylist's mother, Monique, visited Tanya and whispered a prayer over her. More people came—cousins, aunts, old friends from the block. Some stood at her bedside with hands lifted, praying out loud. Others just sat quietly, watching, making sure Tanya knew she wasn't alone. The air felt heavy with love, the kind that presses down on you until it becomes its own kind of medicine.

And Stylist? He never left. He slept in chairs. Brushed her hair. Cleaned her feet when the nurses couldn't stomach it. He held her hand during the most painful dressing changes.

They didn't always talk. Sometimes they just stared out the window, watching clouds float by like spirits. Sometimes she cried. Quietly. But still standing. And he never flinched.

Part IV: Rehab, Rebirth & Return

15.   The Chair, The Cane, The Courage

After two painful months, Tanya was ready for the next chapter: *rehab*. She was non-weight-bearing. Her bones were healing—slowly. Her lungs were stronger. Her body? Scarred. Different. Sacred. But her soul? Still undefeated.

She was wheeled out of Westchester Medical Center like a queen returning to her kingdom. The staff clapped. One nurse cried. A therapist gifted her a journal titled *Still Standing.* And as they strapped her into the van, headed to rehab, Tanya leaned her head back, closed her eyes, and whispered:

"I was crushed, but not killed. Buried, but not broken. And I will walk again—even if I gotta learn how to fly first."

Tanya hadn't cried when the building collapsed. She hadn't cried when her feet were shredded, or when the surgeon said, *"We'll try to save them."* But when they wheeled her into Tarrytown Hall Care Center—tucked in the hills of Tarrytown, New York—and the elevator doors opened to the scent of bleach, old furniture, and fading life? That's when the tears came.

This wasn't what she imagined. Not a rehab center filled with young fighters and buzzing therapy rooms. This was a nursing home.

The woman they paired her with was older than her mother—sweet, frail, and near the end. Tanya looked at her. Then at the oxygen tank. Then she looked at herself. Both feet bandaged. Both legs useless. And she thought: *Am I dying too? What the hell is this?*

She asked for the patient coordinator that same day. "Listen," she said, her voice cool, direct, and impossible to ignore, "I didn't survive a whole-ass building falling on me just to die next to someone's grandma in a twin bed. I need a private room. I need my people. And I need to heal."

They gave her everything she asked for. A private room. They allowed Stylist to sleep over. They allowed her to have visitors nonstop—there were so many visitors. She had candles, music, and her own sheets. She made the room feel like her boutique—minus the lashes and glitter, of course.

But even as her demands were met, something dark lingered. Why were they being so accommodating? Was it pity? Politics? Did they think she'd sue? Did they think she'd die? Either way, Tanya played the game—chess, not checkers.

Tanya at the rehab center with her grandkids

Rehab started the next morning. Her body screamed. Her feet shook. Her spirit nearly buckled. But Tanya? She gripped those parallel bars like a warrior gripping a sword.

From the moment Tanya arrived at rehab, she carried a singular goal in her heart: she needed to go home. Every therapy session, every doctor visit, became a negotiation, a careful dance of persuasion.

She would lean forward in her wheelchair, voice firm, eyes pleading, telling them, "I know I can do this. I need to be home. That's my goal."

The doctors nodded, sympathetic but cautious, reminding her that recovery took time and that pushing too hard could set her back. But Tanya refused to let caution override her resolve. She imagined the familiar rooms of her house, the comforting routines, the independence she craved.

Going home wasn't just a wish—it was a mission, a spark that kept her fighting through pain, through therapy, and through every doubt anyone else might have had about what her body could endure.

Rehabilitation was nothing like the movies. It wasn't a smooth comeback; it was grit, humiliation, and pain stitched together day by day.

Tanya couldn't put weight on her feet for months. Nurses drilled it into her: *"No weight-bearing. Not even to stand up for a second."* So she had to relearn the basics— how to get out of bed, how to balance on a walker, how to move without falling. The first time they sat her up in a chair, sweat poured down her back as if she'd run a marathon.

The nurses showed her and Stylist how to wrap her feet, layer by layer, to keep infection out and swelling down. Stylist's big hands fumbled with the gauze at first, but he kept trying until he got it right. Tanya watched, humbled, grateful, aching.

The pain was constant. Sharp, burning, bone-deep pain that laughed at morphine. Every transfer—from bed to chair, from chair to commode—was a battle.

Then came the parts nobody talks about. The humiliating details of recovery. Bedpans that dug into her skin. She needed help just to wipe, just to change a pad when her period came. No privacy, no dignity—just surrender. Nurses bathing her in warm cloths, washing her hair over a basin, Stylist steadying her so she wouldn't topple. For a woman who once strutted in six-inch heels, showered in perfume, and dressed dancers backstage, it was crushing.

But she didn't quit.

Physical therapy became her battlefield. At first, just flexing her toes sent her into tears. Then, she lifted her legs. Then, standing between parallel bars with therapists on either side. Every inch of progress was agony—but every inch was hers.

It was humbling. It was brutal. But it was also holy. Because in the stripping away of pride, Tanya was being rebuilt. Not just to walk again, but to live again.

Stylist was by her side—always. Her daughters flanked her like bodyguards. And her friends? They came heavy—with food, love, and vibes.

She never ate one plate of rehab food. Not once. Breakfast? Her mother's grits, fried fish, collard greens, devil eggs, and salmon cakes. Lunch? Tasha's soul rolls, fruit salad, and fruit smoothies. Dinner? Raquel's jerk chicken, curry chicken rice, and peas with a cream soda passed behind closed doors. Vanessa brought shrimp alfredo in a Tupperware. And Gina brought her grilled chicken salad from Amici's pizza place, her favorite, and when they weren't bringing food, Stylist kept her with beef, ribs, cabbage, yellow rice, baked ziti, stew, and fish. She definitely ate like the foodie she is.

Stylist bathed her. Styled her hair. Her niece rolled her downstairs to smoke when the nurses turned their heads. Her lashes stayed done. Her hair stayed laid. Even in rehab, Tanya stayed beautiful.

Whispers spread like wildfire through the halls.

"Is she famous?"

"Is there a lawsuit?"

"Who's her lawyer?"

And just like that, Stylist called one—a White Plains shark in a tailored suit. He came. He saw her feet. He heard her story. And he took the case. The lawsuit was real. The pressure was on.

Meanwhile, outside the rehab, the world was unraveling. COVID-19 crept in like a silent assassin. People started coughing. Rooms were quarantined. Staff stopped smiling. Fear replaced routine.

But inside Tanya's room? There was still joy. Still fire. Still hope.

She set a goal: get out before 1st October – Stylist's 40th birthday. That was her North Star.

***

The rehab room was quiet except for the low hum of the movie playing on the small TV, its flickering light casting shadows across the walls. Tanya sat propped in her wheelchair, Stylist beside her, his hand resting lightly on hers. After months of therapy, pain, and frustration, she hadn't even thought about this part of herself—her body's desires, the need for closeness that went beyond comfort.

But today, as the characters on the screen laughed and flirted, warmth spread through her chest. Her hand brushed Stylist's almost accidentally, then lingered. Embarrassment flared immediately—*what was she thinking? Here, in rehab, dependent on others for nearly everything?*

Stylist noticed her hesitation and whispered with a teasing smile, "Wait… how are we gonna do this?"

Tanya blinked at him, startled, then realized the practical problem: the wheelchair. "Well… we'll have to… turn around," she said, trying to keep a straight face.

Tanya pivoted carefully, Stylist's steady hands guiding her, their shared laughter melting any awkwardness. Once aligned, his touch was gentle, patient, and alive with warmth. Each brush of skin, each fleeting glance, reminded her she could still reclaim what she feared lost—her desire, her joy, her freedom.

Encouraged, she leaned closer, fingers tracing the curves of his body, a shiver rippling through her at every touch. Embarrassment and thrill mingled, yet his steady gaze, quiet reassurance, and tender presence invited her to linger. In that intimate space, with laughter and breathless smiles weaving between them, Tanya felt truly seen, cherished, and safe.

By the time the movie ended, Tanya's heart was racing, her cheeks still warm with a combination of desire and shame. Yet underneath it all was a quiet, powerful realization: even here, in the sterile halls of rehab, she could reclaim parts of herself she had feared lost. She could feel, she could want, she could be fully alive—and Stylist would be there to honor that, every step of the way.

***

Every day, she pushed:

- Leg lifts with tears in her eyes.

- Stationary bikes with blood in her socks.

- Crying at night, smiling in the morning.

- Begging God. Cursing life. Loving Stylist.

Rehab had already tested Tanya in ways she never imagined—her legs stiff and scarred, her spirit often weary. She celebrated the small victories, like standing for a few seconds without support or taking one shaky step with the walker. Yet one day stood out above all the rest, a day that shook her to the core and reminded her why she had to keep pushing.

Stylist insisted on taking her to the Puerto Rican Day Parade. At first, she was grateful for the fresh air, the thrum of music, the bright colors swirling around her. But when gunshots cracked through the crowd, everything changed.

Puerto Rican Day

Panic exploded, people screaming and running, and in that split second, Stylist darted across the street, forgetting she couldn't run. Trapped in her wheelchair, her heart froze as the stampede surged. Tasha's boyfriend, Mikai, flung himself in front of her, shielding her from being trampled.

Moments later, Stylist came rushing back, grabbing the chair. "I got her, I got her!" he cried, wheeling her toward the car.

When they were finally safe, Tanya's fear turned into fury. "Don't you ever leave me like that again!" she shouted, tears streaming down her face. "Take me back to rehab right now—I can't do this. I can't be out here like this. I felt helpless, Stylist. Do you hear me? Helpless."

Stylist hung his head, guilt written all over his face. "I just wanted you to feel normal again," he whispered.

Her voice softened but carried a hard edge. "Normal? Normal is walking. Normal is not having to depend on somebody to save me when the world turns upside down. I want that back."

That night in rehab, Tanya couldn't sleep. The chaos of the parade replayed in her mind over and over. But instead of breaking her, it lit a fire inside her. She made herself a promise: she would fight harder, push past the pain, and reclaim her independence. No more feeling helpless. That day at the parade became the turning point—the day she realized walking again wasn't just about healing her body. It was about taking her power back.

When Tanya was alone in her rehab room, she discovered a small ritual that became hers alone. Carefully, she would try to shift her weight, pressing down on her feet, testing for pain.

At first, every step was tentative, her body screaming in protest, but slowly—miraculously—she realized she could stand without the sharp sting that had haunted her for months. Heart pounding with excitement, she began to take a few steps, then a few more, savoring the freedom of each movement.

She didn't tell anyone—not the nurses, not Stylist, not her friends—because she wanted this victory to be hers, a secret triumph that would one day surprise them all and remind them just how strong she really was.

The day finally came when Tanya could no longer contain her secret. Stylist had wheeled her into the therapy room, chatting with a nurse as she pretended to need help adjusting her brace. Then, with a deep breath and a pounding heart, she let go of the wheelchair and took a confident step forward.

Stylist froze, eyes wide, as she took another, then another, each one steadier than the last. The nurse gasped, clapping her hands in delight, and Stylist's face lit up with a mixture of shock and pride.

"Tanya… you—how—?" he stammered, nearly at a loss for words.

She laughed, a triumphant, relieved sound, and said, "I wanted it to be a surprise."

Her heart raced with pride as she looked at Stylist, a triumphant smile spreading across her face. "See? I told you I could do it," she said, her voice bright with excitement.

Stylist's eyes widened, a mix of disbelief and awe, and he quickly pulled out his phone. "We need to call your doctor—let him know you can stand on your own. Let's get the paperwork started," he said, practically bouncing with joy.

Tanya grinned at the thought: if all went well, she could be released by October 1st—Stylist's birthday. The idea of walking out of rehab on that special day, fully independent and celebrated by the man who had supported her every step, made her chest swell with pride and anticipation.

In that moment, every hour of pain, frustration, and uncertainty felt worth it—Tanya had reclaimed her independence, and the joy on their faces made the secret all the sweeter.

On the day of Stylist's birthday, she stood—really stood. Her feet still healing, her bones still aching. But she did it. A walker in hand. Determination in her blood.

"Happy birthday, baby," she said. "I'm coming home."

Tanya didn't just survive. She returned stronger. From the rubble of a boutique to a throne of resilience. From blood-stained floors to clean-cut lawsuits. From screams for help to praise from trauma surgeons—she became a living testimony.

She didn't just heal. She reminded the world: some women were built from concrete, not glass. And Tanya? She didn't crack. She shined.

Tanya had dreamed of this day for months: the day she could finally leave the rehab center and return to her own home.

Every therapy session, every meeting with the doctors felt like a negotiation, a battle of wills. *"I need to be home,"* she told them over and over, her voice steady but desperate. She wanted her own bed. Her own walls. Her own peace. Not the fluorescent lights and call buttons of a facility. Home was her finish line. Home was her medicine.

And after rounds of testing, endless patience, and stubborn determination, the doctors finally agreed. Her release date was set for October 1st—Stylist's birthday.

16.   Back to Home

The irony wasn't lost on her. The man who had carried her through the darkest nights, who had wrapped her bandages with shaking hands, now shared his birthday with her new beginning. It felt like a gift—a sign.

***

On the way back from rehab, the long drive proved to be the much-needed escape Tanya and Stylist needed. While driving through the busy roads, Stylist told her that another surprise awaited her. She couldn't contain her excitement over the news. She wanted to know the details, but he hadn't wanted to tell her ahead of time. The surprise would mean more if she discovered it all at once.

After nearly an hour, the city began to thin out—tall buildings giving way to quiet neighborhoods and the soft hum of sprinklers misting lawns.

Tanya glanced out the window, trying to guess where they were headed. Stylist only smiled.

"Close your eyes," he said suddenly, after some time.

She hesitated, laughing nervously. "Now? While you're driving?"

"Trust me," he said with that familiar warmth in his voice. "It's part of the surprise."

He slowed the car to a stop at the curb, reached over gently, and tied a soft blindfold around her eyes. "No peeking," he murmured. "You'll see everything in just a few more minutes."

She could feel the cool brush of fabric and the faint tremor of excitement in her chest.

The car door opened; the outside air was fresh and bright. She heard the sound of the wheelchair unfolding, the click of its frame locking into place. Then his hands— steady, careful—helped her out, easing her into the seat.

"Almost there," he said, wheeling her forward. The small bumps of the curb jolted beneath her, but she didn't mind. The rhythmic squeak of the wheels and the soft crunch of gravel became the music of anticipation. She had no idea what was going on, but she was having positive vibes about the whole aura.

"Not yet," he teased, as they reached the front steps. He wheeled her carefully up toward the door. The wheels of her chair shook over the uneven pavement—but her spirit didn't.

The door's hinges gave a faint groan as he pushed it open, sunlight spilling across the floor. Only then did he lift the blindfold away.

"Tadaa! This," he said softly, watching her face, "is your new home."

It was indeed her new home, and she was very happy to see it. Her face glowed with delight, and she couldn't stop smiling.

"I love this wonderful surprise…"

Every bump was a reminder of how far she had come, every turn a small victory against the months of pain and rehab. This wasn't just a new address. It was a resurrection, a reclaiming of life on her own terms.

For a moment, Tanya just stood there, breath caught, her gaze sweeping over the empty rooms. It wasn't polished or perfect—not yet. The walls needed fresh sheetrock, the floors begged for wax, and every appliance was coated in dust. The stove and refrigerator would require a thorough scrubbing, while the windows were streaked with years of neglect. It was, in every sense of the word, a fixer-upper.

But beneath the rough edges lay promise. The high ceilings echoed with possibility, and the bare walls seemed to invite her touch. It wasn't just a house; it was a place waiting for her laughter, her warmth, her life. And though it needed work, it was hers!

While she had been fighting for her life inside a trauma ward, Stylist had been quietly building a sanctuary for her on the outside. He bought a house—a whole new home.

Not a fancy condo or luxury apartment—this was a real home. Rooms with character, walls waiting to tell new stories, and windows desperate to let light pour in. It was raw. It was unfinished. But it was theirs.

The triumphant moment of return she had imagined to be smooth wasn't as she expected. The house, though new, greeted her with silence—quiet, stale, and slightly disarrayed from months of absence. Dust clung to surfaces, the air smelled still, and everything seemed heavier. She just stared around her as the weight of "starting over" pressed down on her chest.

But shortly after she came home, her friends and family showed up like an army of angels—masks on, cleaning supplies in hand, hearts wide open, ready to restore her world.

Alberta scrubbed the windows until sunlight danced across the panes, as if washing away the shadows of the past.

And she scrubbed the stove until it gleamed like her spirit—shining, resilient, untouchable.

Manny wiped down the walls, hung framed pictures of laughter and love, and whispered blessings into every corner.

Her daughters fluffed pillows and made the beds with sheets that smelled of lavender, renewal, and hope. Her mother arrived with soul food, old-school gospel echoing through the rooms, filling the air with comfort and healing.

Her sons played their part alongside Stylist. They moved the heavy furniture, built the beds, carried the washer and dryer to the laundry building, installed vanities, stripped & waxed the floors, and did all the heavy-duty work.

Her friends and family proved to be the best support system. She wasn't left alone in reclaiming it. The people came—her people. Friends poured in, one by one, like soldiers reporting for duty.

Pots and pans clattered in the kitchen. The scent of garlic and onions filled the air. Laughter floated down the hallways as trash bags filled, shelves were dusted, and furniture was shifted back into place. Someone popped open drinks, while someone else played music softly from their phone. Slowly, room by room, her house came alive again.

It wasn't just cleaning—it was restoration. It was love in motion. Each sweep of the broom, each meal on the stove, each hug in passing stitched Tanya's spirit back together.

The walls that had sat empty for years now hummed with life, echoing the sound of a woman reclaiming not just her space—but herself.

This wasn't just a move-in. It was a rebirth—a celebration of survival, strength, and the quiet power of building a life from the ashes. Every wall, every corner, every smell of food and sunshine whispered: You are home. You are whole. You are unstoppable.

But the reality didn't hide for long. Two surgical boots. One walker. A shower chair. A wheelchair that barely fit through doorways. And steps. Too many steps.

Some mornings, she'd wake up downstairs, stuck—waiting for someone to help her rise. Other mornings, she tried to crawl on her own, dragging her dignity behind her, breath ragged, feet aching, but soul unbreakable.

During long stretches of solitude, Tanya started writing. Words poured out—her story, her pain, her questions. *Why me? Why that building? Why survive? Why was I left alive when everything else collapsed?*

She talked with her lawyer, but his voice didn't bring the comfort she hoped for. He told her the lawsuit might not stick. They were calling it "an act of God"—rain, thunder, lightning—a natural disaster. And because COVID-19 had shut the courts down, everything was on hold.

Tanya didn't crumble. She'd already survived worse. She stayed busy with weekly doctor visits to clean and check her wounds and what seemed like endless rehab appointments—sometimes her mom drove, sometimes Stylist, sometimes her daughters.

Music playing in the background, painkillers numbing her legs, while creativity awakened her soul. She started doodling. Little affirmations. Raw sketches. Pieces of a future memoir she already saw in her dreams.

She set up a small hustle again, selling shapewear and birthday outfits to both old and new clients. Her vendors never forgot her hustle, and her people never stopped buying.

COVID kept the world apart. But Tanya's house stayed full. Love poured in through every window, every door, every laugh: Friends brought flowers, food, and faith. TikToks, jokes, and dance challenges filled the living room, breaking the silence of recovery.

Her daughters braided her hair, painted her toes, and laughed at the news as if the world outside could never touch them.

Her porch became a sanctuary, the place people came to recharge, to breathe, to be reminded that life—messy, hard, beautiful—was still worth living.

Even in limitation, Tanya found abundance. Even in pain, she found purpose. The world had slowed, but she had not stopped.

Soon, Tanya felt settled. Once steady, she began to carve out her own rhythm at home. What could have felt like confinement slowly revealed itself as something different— a canvas—a space where she could rediscover herself without the noise of the outside world.

She leaned into quiet joys. Arts and crafts became a form of therapy, with each project serving as a meditation. Diamond painting, with its tiny shimmering beads, drew her in. She spent hours patiently piecing together portraits of her grandchildren, each sparkle a reminder of legacy, of love, of why she fought so hard to survive. Finished canvases glowed from her walls—faces of her babies, preserved in glittering detail, watching over her.

Her creativity didn't stop there. She looked around her house with fresh eyes and saw possibilities. One project at a time, she began to transform her space. She reupholstered her dining room chairs in a rich blue suede—her hands steadying, her vision sharpening with every staple and every smooth pull of fabric. The simple change brought elegance into the room, a touch of the sophistication she had always dreamed of.

And then, one day, she found herself back in the kitchen. Even making dinner felt like a mountain. She stood in the kitchen staring at a pan, trying to remember how long chicken needed to cook.

Depression nipped at her, whispering, "You're not strong enough." But Tanya kept repeating out loud: "I came too far to turn back. Push forward, Tanya. Push forward."

At first, it was just small meals—boiling pasta, frying eggs. Even that had felt huge. Tanya used a walker with a small built-in seat, her constant companion in the kitchen. She could stand for about ten minutes at a time before the ache in her legs grew too sharp to ignore. Then she'd sit, rest, breathe through the sting of frustration, and wait until her strength crept back. Ten minutes up. Ten minutes down. Again and again.

Sometimes she'd grip the counter until her knuckles whitened, muttering under her breath when a pan proved too heavy or a pot of water sloshed over the rim. The simplest motions—balancing the knife, turning a spoon—demanded patience she didn't always have. There were moments of anger and annoyance. She'd get exasperated at her own body for betraying her. Amid this, sometimes, her eyes would glisten without warning.

But she kept at it. Trying and managing bit by bit. Slowly, she gained more strength, more confidence, and the familiar routine returned. The chopping, the sizzling, the stirring. The kitchen filled with aromas of garlic, peppers, and seasoned meats—the kind of smells that meant family, celebration, and life. Each dish was more than food; it was a declaration: *I am still here.*

* * *

Tanya was trying to fit herself back into her old, normal lifestyle. Even amidst the challenges of Covid—when the outside world felt frozen, uncertain, and heavy—she let her home become a refuge of light.

The return of her children layered that joy with something deeper. Just three weeks before Tanya left the rehab that felt like a nursing home, her eldest son, Tamel, walked back through the doors, newly released from prison. Four months later, Dazjohn followed. Their homecoming was more than a reunion—it was a rebirth of family. Their presence brought a cadence, a warmth, a sense of wholeness she had longed for while stuck in hospital beds and rehab halls.

The house, once hollow, empty, and shushed, now pulsed with life—music, conversation, vibrance, and laughter echoing against the walls she had fought so hard to return to.

***

Life after being home was not without challenges, but Tanya carried herself differently now. Every step she took—whether with crutches, a walker, or her wheelchair—was proof that she had survived the unthinkable.

Still, survival came with shadows. Her weariness was more than just anxiety. It weighed heavily on her, and she doubted it was PTSD. Certainly it was, but she wasn't sure until one day when she sat by the window. The day was dark and cloudy. Wind gusts carried gloom and dust. Soon, it started pouring heavily.

Something about the steady drumming on the windows pulled her back to darker memories she tried not to revisit.

Rain made her blue, and on those dull, gray days, her body ached more, her spirit sagged, and the silence of the house seemed to echo louder than usual. Her loneliness gnawed at her.

When she was around people—friends dropping by, a phone call, a TV humming in the background—she felt lighter, almost normal. As long as something was happening, she didn't have time to feel. But in her quiet, alone moments, the melancholy would seep in slowly, like cold air through a crack in the door. She'd catch herself staring at nothing, lost between gratitude for being alive and the weight of what she'd endured.

Even so, her home became both sanctuary and stage: a place where she healed, created, laughed, and rediscovered herself. She found herself leaning into her crafts, cooking, and small joys with a gratitude that deepened everything she touched.

Her children and grandchildren kept the house buzzing—birthdays, Sunday dinners, and quiet visits that reminded her she was never alone. Friends dropped in often, not just to help but to sit, laugh, and share life. Stylist, steady at her side, continued to be her anchor, while her daughters became her partners in both care and joy.

To mark her full reintegration into the community, her daughters, Stylist, her mother, and close friends organized a welcome-home party at the Underwear Factory.

The welcome-home party had marked a freshening point—it was not just the end of rehab, but the beginning of a lively chapter. Life after being home was about more than recovery. It was about embracing resilience as her identity, joy as her medicine, and love as her constant.

The celebration was a feast of love and gratitude: food, desserts, drinks, photos, and giggles everywhere. Everyone attended, even some of the firefighters who had once helped her, adding to the sense of community and care that had surrounded her throughout her journey.

That day, Tanya felt truly at home—celebrated, supported, and connected to the people who had never let her face recovery alone. Surrounded by family, friends, and the simple joys of her own space, she knew that this was more than a return home.

It was a reclaiming of life, a testament to resilience, and a celebration of love that carried her through every challenge.

17.   Returning to Life

Her return was celebrated, cherished, and shared. Everyone was happy and was somewhat back to normal life, but for Tanya, the real work had just begun: her physical therapy.

Four times a week, Tanya pushed herself through grueling sessions, determined to reclaim her independence. Every milestone, no matter how small, felt monumental—graduating from the wheelchair to a chair walker, then finally taking steps with a cane.

Each victory was a quiet triumph, fueling her determination to stand tall again, fully and fearlessly. And her progress did not go unnoticed. Community invitations began trickling in, and Tanya was greeted with warmth, recognition, and admiration.

She attended the Mayor's Ball and the Fireman's Association Ball, walking into rooms filled with applause, smiles, and nods of respect. At the Fireman's Ball, she had the honor of presenting awards to the very firefighters who had pulled her from the rubble—men who had been her lifeline through the darkest hours.

Cane in hand but heart strong, she felt a profound mix of gratitude and empowerment. These were not just ceremonies; they were celebrations of resilience, courage, and the unbreakable human spirit.

"I'll never forget what it felt like—six hours buried beneath concrete, unsure if I'd ever see daylight again. When the firefighters pulled me out, they didn't just save my body—they rescued my spirit."

Tanya's voice, her message, touched many ears and several hearts.

"Months later, I'm having the honor of standing beside them at an award ceremony. The black I'm wearing is a symbol of my healing."

Tanya remembers the weight of that moment: the applause, the cameras, the emotions she couldn't fully put into words. But what stayed with her the most was the quiet gratitude in her heart.

Standing between those brave men, she wasn't just a survivor—she was living proof that even in the darkest moments, light finds a way through.

***

Evenings at home became her sanctuary. She reflected on her journey—from the uncertainty and pain of hospital halls to the vibrant, laughter-filled energy of her living room, surrounded by friends, family, and Stylist's steady support.

Every meal shared, every word of encouragement, every gentle push from her therapist reminded her that life could still be beautiful after devastation. Tanya had not only survived—she had returned to life fully, reclaiming her strength, independence, and rightful place in the community she loved.

Gradually, she began reclaiming herself. Little by little, the world started opening back up to her. She began going out with friends on her own—no Stylist, no mom—just her, her cane, and her wheelchair.

Each outing, no matter how insignificant, felt like a personal triumph. Sitting at a café, laughing until her cheeks hurt, rolling through the park with music in her ears—these moments reminded her of who she used to be, and who she was becoming again. The small things became her victories.

She even started driving by herself; the hum of the engine, the steering wheel beneath her hands, the control over the pedals, felt like freedom itself. Every mile, every attempt stitched another piece of her back together.

One morning, she woke up with the heaviness pressing on her. She didn't want to get out of bed, but forced herself to lace up her sneakers and take a walk.

The refreshing breeze on Tanya's face reminded her—*you're still alive*.

She was rebuilding her life, one shaky step at a time. It may not look like much to anyone else, but for her, every day was a battle won.

***

One miserable day, her close friend Ann lost her aunt. Tanya, despite the weight of her own pain, insisted on being there. With *Hurricane*—the name she had given her walker—by her side, Tanya attended the funeral.

She was being very emotional because she hadn't been in this type of environment for a long time. Nervously driving to Beacon, when she arrived, she called Ann. She came to the parking lot, took her walker out, and they proceeded to go into the church. Ann helped her into the funeral, steadying her with quiet encouragement.

The service was beautiful. The repass, even better. Amidst the grief and soft murmurs of condolences, Tanya met Ann's cousin. Something clicked—not romantic, not forced, just real. They started texting, talking, healing.

The cousin often prayed with her and wouldn't forget to remind her that she's strong and resilient. He frequently said it.

"You're beautiful, Tanya. You didn't survive for nothing."

"God spared you for a purpose. Now go find your why."

"You're smart and capable. You're not born to be bound."

Between whispered *amens,* his faith was steady, grounding Tanya when her own hope wavered. Whenever Tanya doubted herself or stared too long at her scars, his voice would break through the noise.

"Your willpower is incredible and inspirational."

"You can overcome anything you've set your mind to."

That's when the shift happened. His words sank deep, especially on the nights when pain and fear kept her awake. Tanya stopped waiting for the lawsuit. Stopped hoping for courtrooms and cash. Instead, she focused on the moment. She couldn't walk fast. She couldn't stand long. But she could create. She could share. She could live.

Disability checks and hustle money kept her afloat. Loyal customers came through for her shapewear, lashes, and birthday outfits—even when boutiques were shut down.

And every time someone asked, "How'd you survive that?" She smiled, held her head high, and replied, "Because love never left me. And I never left myself."

Tanya's house might've had stairs, pain, and uncertainty. But it also had music. It had warmth. It had purpose etched into every corner and promise stitched into every chair she reupholstered.

Her old life may have collapsed—but her new one? It was being built on unshakable faith, resilience, and a determination that no disaster could ever steal.

***

The hairdresser's chair has always been Tanya's safe place. That day, she went in hoping to feel beautiful again. And as the dresser's hands worked through her hair, she laughed at her stories, almost forgetting the battles of the past year.

But the merriment was temporary. A bubble that was burst by a phone call. Tanya's buzzing phone gave disconcerting vibes.

The voice on the other end was shaky and shattered her calm. It was Aunt Eunice.

"Ta… Tanya… something happened to Ebony."

Confused, she asked, "Ebony who? My daughter, or my husband?"

"Your husband, crazy! Something happened."

"Something happened, like what?" Tanya asked.

But Aunt Eunice didn't know. "I'm not sure."

"Okay… I'm at the hairdresser's, let me call you back."

Her heart dropped at the unclear message. She sat unmoving, hair half-done, mind racing. *What do you mean, something happened? Is he hurt? Is he gone? Why can't they just tell me?*

Hours passed in distress and ambiguity. The incomplete information created a weird chaos that wasn't settling at any point.

While Patricia, her stylist, wrapped up her work, Tanya's phone rang again and again—calls from her children, her sister-in-law, all with the same news. Ebony had been found in an apartment on Carol Street—a fiend's place.

Later, the phone rang again.

"Is this Miss Cooper?"

The name caught her off guard. Nobody had called her that since 2012, when Ebony and she were divorced.

"This is the coroner's office… Ebony was found deceased. We need someone to identify the body. You're listed as next of kin."

Tanya gripped the phone so tight that her knuckles whitened. For a few seconds, she couldn't comprehend what had happened. What she listened to and what she's gonna do.

She asked a hundred questions, desperate for answers. The coroner explained that an autopsy would be performed, and at that time, more details could be divulged. But before that, the body needed to be identified.

Barely breathing, Tanya whispered, "Okay."

On the blank slate of her mind, questions flooded that seemingly had no answers. *How? Why me? He's been with another woman for 12 years. He even had a son with her. Why am I the one they're calling?*

After having 101 questions that ran through her mind, she understood it. She got it. Ebony was her husband. She had spent half her life with him. She learned this thing called life with him. Of course, she was next of kin; of course, she was notified. And so she obliged.

***

Ebony died on September 11[th,] 2020, of a fentanyl overdose. Someone had laced his cocaine with it. His life had turned down a road far different from the one he once shared with Tanya and his children—his family.

After separating from his son's mother, he succumbed to the streets. Still, when he wasn't outside, he often stayed with his daughter, Ebony. He always said he was coming back to get his family.

Tanya's thoughts spiraled to a recent encounter. A memory she didn't know would turn so heartfelt. Just days before his death, Tanya had seen him. He was standing in front of the barbershop where he worked.

It was a Wednesday. She drove past and jokingly called out of her car window: "Yo EB! You know you don't wear white. Go take those white jeans off. You know white makes you look skinny."

Ebony laughed back and shouted, "OK TANZ, I KNOW I AM!"

That moment stayed with her—always.

***

Gathering her children was the most challenging part for Tanya. They looked at her, expecting answers she didn't have.

The air was heavy, as if everyone already knew something was terribly wrong. She looked at them and said, "Tamel, Dazjohn… your father is gone."

The room cracked open with grief. It erupted. Tamel punched the wall, his face twisted in pain. Dazjohn sat down hard, shaking his head, tears streaming silently.

Tamel didn't speak, but his inner thoughts could be heard: "How could this happen? Why didn't anyone tell us sooner? I need to know what happened. I can't just sit here."

Dazjohn said it out loud: "No… no… this can't be real. I just saw him. I just heard his voice. Pops… how could you leave us like this?"

The boys wanted to go into the streets to find answers themselves. Tanya wanted to stop them, but also understood their rage.

She thought helplessly, *How do I comfort them when I'm breaking too?*

The girls were shocked and silent, each one swirling into her own thoughts. Emani's thought: *My heart is breaking. Pop's gone? How do I breathe without him? Who's going to cheer me on now?*

Ebony's thought: *Daddy was supposed to be here for us, for my children. To see Coah. Like forever. I feel lost. I want to scream, but all I can do is cry. Pops, your girls will always love & miss you so much…*

All four children promised themselves: *we have to keep his memory alive!*

And as all of them stood together in the blue dining room, they also tried to piece together the fragments. *Who was he with? Where was he? What happened? Why?*

No one knew anything.

***

The new day rose with the same weariness as yesterday. Sadness and rage filled the atmosphere. Tanya walked into the coroner's office with all four children by her side. The smell of antiseptic and silence was suffocating. It was a very heart-wrenching moment for them.

When they revealed the body, her heart stopped. Ebony lay still. Tamel gripped his mother's arm so tightly it hurt. His tears came fast. He couldn't hold them back.

Chokingly, he said, "That's him… that's Pops."

Inside, he thought, *This isn't real. I shouldn't be here. I shouldn't be seeing this. But I have to be strong for Ma. I can't let her stand here alone.*

On the other hand, Tanya's inner thoughts were: *I wish I could take this memory from my son, erase it from his eyes. No child should have to see their father this way.*

Ebony, though unmoving and lifeless, looked perfect—like he was only asleep. He looked peaceful, like all the chaos had finally quieted.

***

Word spread quickly through the community—Ebony was gone. Some pushed for a grand funeral, but Ebony was Muslim. Tradition called for simplicity and a swift burial.

"We'll honor him the right way," Tanya told her children.

Still, the pressure came from every direction—whispers, opinions, demands. But what came from others didn't matter. Tanya held firm. *This isn't about what people want,* she thought. *This is about respecting who he was.*

Ebony's brothers, sisters, and closest loved ones gathered for a simple, heartfelt ceremony. There were no frills, no excess—just tears, prayers, and silence. It was exactly what it needed to be.

The decision was made for cremation, a difficult decision, but one they felt was right. His ashes were buried at Hyde Park Cemetery, among Tanya's grandparents and many relatives.

Dazjohn thought, *It feels strange, Pops being in ashes instead of a casket. But maybe this way, he's closer to us. Maybe this way, he's free.*

At Hyde Park Cemetery, Tanya stood surrounded by generations of her family. Her grandparents and other family members rested there. Now, so did Ebony.

She whispered a prayer—not only for him, but for her children, and for herself. *Oh Allah... My heart is heavy, and my spirit trembles under the weight of this loss. You called their father home so suddenly, and though I trust Your will, the pain still cuts deep. I come to You not only for myself, but for my children — the pieces of my heart walking this earth.*

Wrap us in Your arms, ALLAH. Where I fall short, be their comfort. Where I am weak, be their strength. Let them feel their father's love in the quiet moments, in the memories that make them smile, and in the legacy he left behind.

Help me guide them with patience, wisdom, and grace. Keep their hearts soft, even as they grieve. Remind them that they are never alone, for You walk beside them, and I am here, always.

Heal the cracks in our souls, ALLAH. Replace sorrow with peace, confusion with clarity, and pain with purpose.

Let our family's story be one of resilience, love, and unshakable faith.

And for me, ALLAH, give me the courage to keep standing, the strength to keep leading, and the tenderness to keep loving them through it all.

In Your name, I pray. Ameen.

18.   The Comeback Queen

Even in limitation, Tanya discovered abundance. Even in pain, she uncovered purpose. The world slowed down, but Tanya refused to stop.

Tanya had not only survived; she had returned to life fully, gradually regaining her strength, independence, and place in the community she loved.

There were days the weight of it all tried to pull her under, but she kept reminding herself of the woman she had always been: a fighter, a mother, a survivor.

She started to pour back into me-time—spas, self-care, FaceTiming her children and grandchildren, letting their voices remind her why she couldn't quit. Healing wasn't just physical—it was spiritual.

Reclaiming her life meant rewriting her story. She refused to let that collapse be the end of her. Instead, it became the beginning of her rise. She found joy again in the little things, laughter in her family's voices, and love in every moment she chose herself.

For a few years, Tanya focused on readjusting — learning how to listen to her body, how to breathe through the pain, and how to find joy in stillness. It wasn't easy for someone who was used to being on the move, creating, serving, and inspiring others. But even in stillness, her spirit refused to sit still.

This battle could have broken her, but all it did was reveal the beauty of her strength.

The collapse had stolen so much from Tanya—her health, her mobility, her sense of certainty. But it had not stolen her vision. When she and Stylist won that little fixer-upper in Hyde Park, it felt like a declaration: we are still building.

***

It was one fine day when Stylist walked in and said to Tanya, "Let's go look at this property in Hyde Park."

She blinked. "Hyde Park? Out of the city? Ain't nobody wants no property in Hyde Park. There ain't shit in Hyde Park."

They drove up anyway—windows down, music low, air thick with possibility. It was a ride to Hyde Park for an auction. *Just to look,* they said. Just to see what was out there. But fate had a way of turning "just to see" into a new chapter.

In that crowded auction room, their paddle went up, and their lives took another turn. They won a house tucked away on Reservoir Road — quiet, green, and full of possibilities. The house was rough—trees strangling the yard and old pipes rusted underground.

They jumped in right away, determined to bring the house up to par. Tanya and Stylist dreamed of turning it into a three-bedroom, two-bath home. They hired an architect, poured over blueprints, and spent long nights talking about layouts and finishes, picturing family gatherings and fresh starts. And submitted everything to the town.

Then came the first blow. The zoning board's answer was firm: "Denied." The town of Hyde Park refused to budge on floor plans.

What started with excitement turned into exhaustion. Renovations became a circus. Permits got delayed, contractors disappeared, and old zoning laws turned simple plans into headaches. What was meant to be a new chapter started to feel like another fight.

Back and forth.

Edit after edit.

Revision after revision.

Each time they adjusted the plans, the town came back with another "no." Hope turned into months of frustration. It felt personal — like every effort to rebuild was being rejected. The meetings grew tense, the excitement faded, and Tanya began to wonder if they had made a mistake.

The house, they were told, was *grandfathered in* as a two-bedroom, one-bath — and there would be no changing that.

Each "no" stung, but each setback taught them something — about patience, about process, about letting go when it's time.

There were nights she sat quietly, looking at the plans spread across the table, asking herself if maybe this was a sign to let go. The weight of disappointment felt familiar — another battle she didn't ask for but had to face.

Eventually, they made the difficult decision to sell the property. But life has a way of turning losses into lessons. When the sale went through, the house sold for twice what they paid.

It wasn't the dream home they built on paper — but it was a reminder that even when something doesn't go as planned, it can still lead to gain.

That house, that process, that "no" — it wasn't a waste. It was a blueprint for patience, resilience, and faith. Because sometimes, God's redirection is still construction.

God always has ways. He sent someone. That's how John from Amity Construction appeared—boots dusty, clipboard in hand, blueprints ready. His plans weren't enough for the town, but his presence shifted something bigger. He was a worker who had been excavating the backyard.

Over coffee, he confessed, "I own Oakwood Plaza. We need to bring it back to life. And you can do it. I'll give you a storefront."

Tanya laughed bitterly. "I'm still in physical therapy, John. I can't even walk a block without this walker."

But John pressed. "You're already running a business out of your house. Let me make it easier. No rent for the first year. Fix it up. Make it her own."

"A boutique? Again? I'm not opening another boutique. That chapter's closed. I've been there, done that."

But the offer? Too good to ignore. Too tempting to refuse. After several days of debating and pondering, Tanya decided to accept it.

The next few months consisted of getting in touch with her previous vendors and shopping for new furniture and fixtures.

The store had been vacant for over seven years; it needed some work of its own, and so the task began. Soon, Stylist and his friend Donell transformed the empty suite into something new: Hardwood floors, the color of rich coffee. And walls were painted in a soft, warm pink.

Tanya sat in the doorway with her walker, watching her new beginning take shape. She moved her products there. At first, it was just for pick-ups. A quiet spot to store inventory away from home, to meet clients safely, to stay busy without overextending herself. But customers kept coming, and coming, and coming.

And one day, she stood in the middle of that bare little storefront—paint-stained floors, half-stocked shelves, the faint smell of new beginnings and said, "Let's open it. For real this time."

They blew life into that small space right at the end of Covid. When it opened, it wasn't perfect timing. It was 2020. The world hadn't completely opened its eyes; it had been shut down. But Tanya refused to let fear smother her fire. She hosted a grand opening anyway—mask on, sanitizer at the door, but still cakes on trays, chilled drinks, and gift bags for every woman who came.

"I'm back," she told them. "We're back."

In December 2021, Hotties Boutique reopened. New location. New vision. Same unbreakable spirit.

And it's been thriving ever since. Not just because of the clothes. Not because of the shapewear, accessories, or lashes. But because of the vibe.

Photo shoot for Hotties Boutique, grand reopening
From left to right: Brianna, Raquel, Aja, Benetta, & Ellie
Tonya in the middle

From left to right: Aja, Brianna, Ebony, Raquel, Benetta, Ellie

At Hotties Boutique, women walk in and feel like family. Tanya greets them with warmth—sometimes a plate of food, sometimes a cold drink, always a smile. She listens. Encourages. Reminds them that they're still beautiful. Still worthy. Still standing.

Because whatever they're going through—she's been through challenges as well, and she's living proof that beauty can rise from rubble.

Every rack of clothes, every folded garment, every mirror on the wall speaks of resilience. The space isn't just a shop—it's a sanctuary. A sisterhood. A soft landing for women rediscovering themselves.

When someone walks in feeling unsure, broken, or insecure, Tanya says the same thing she once said to herself: "You're not done. You're just getting started."

From buried alive to boutique boss, Tanya didn't just survive—she transformed. She rebuilt. She rose. And now she reigns. Again.

All this time, Ebony, her elder daughter, was by her side, though hesitant. She had just trained in permanent makeup—microblading, brows, lip blushing—but doubt clung to her.

"Mom, I'm not ready," she whispered one afternoon. Tanya's reply was sharp but loving. "Scared money doesn't make money. Let's go. We got shit to do."

Her youngest, Emani, had just finished a lash course, ready to offer individual lashes. For a time, it was perfect:

the three of them together, a one-stop shop for women, daughters building alongside their mother.

Tanya with her beautiful daughters – Ebony & Emani

Women came for shapewear, brows, and lashes—and left with confidence stitched back into their spirit.

But not every dream lasts the same. Emani realized lashes weren't for her, choosing a career in corrections instead.

Tanya kissed her cheek and told her, "Baby, there's beauty in all battles—even the battles that lead you somewhere else."

It left Tanya and Ebony to hold down the fort. And they did. Together, they built something steady. By 2023, the boutique had become more than a store—it was a refuge. Women walked in for appointments but stayed for conversation, for encouragement, for healing.

Then, in April 2023, joy entered in the form of a baby boy: Ebony's son, Coah. From the moment he was born, he was part of the boutique. A bassinet in the corner, soft coos between clients, little giggles echoing through the walls that Tanya and Stylist had fought so hard to paint.

Tanya had 7 grandchildren already, but there was something different about Coah. She always said, "When your daughter has a baby, it's like your heart is born all over again."

The bond between them was unshakable. Tanya was called "Yaya" by him. His tiny arms reached for her every time he saw her. She adored him with a love that felt brand-new, and he adored her right back.

While Ebony worked, Yaya and Coah built their own rhythm—her laughter filling the shop as she bounced him on her knee, his baby hands reaching for her jewelry, his presence softening even the hardest days. He wasn't just her grandson; he was her heartbeat outside her body.

Tanya & Coah

There was something sacred about watching her daughter raise a child. It was as if the universe had given Tanya a second chance to be a mother again, this time with wisdom, patience, and a joy that only comes after surviving storms.

Tanya, Ebony, & Coah

By 2024, the boutique would no longer be just Tanya's comeback. It was a family legacy. Hardwood floors and pink walls held the sound of three generations—mother, daughter, and grandson—creating something larger than themselves.

By 2025, Tanya could look at her boutique and see not just survival, but legacy. From rubble to reopening, from lawsuits denied to grand openings in a pandemic, from physical therapy to hardwood floors, from fear to faith—she had built more than walls.

She had built a future.

The walls of the boutique had seen it all—panic, anxiety, poise, passion, confidence, devotion, sweat, tears, laughter, and new beginnings.

It wasn't the kind of legacy written in boardrooms or bank accounts. It was a legacy of grit. Of showing her children—and now her grandchildren—that no matter what life tried to take away, a woman could rise again.

Tanya thought back to the collapse, to the rubble and pain, to the endless days of physical therapy when she questioned if she'd ever walk normally again. Yet here she was, not only walking but carrying others with her—her daughters, her customers, her community.

Ebony worked beside her now, steady and strong. The shy girl who once trembled at the thought of taking on clients had blossomed into a confident businesswoman, her hands reshaping brows and lips while her spirit reshaped her own future.

Tanya often told her, "Baby, you were scared, but you did it anyway. That's what strength looks like."

And the legacy wasn't just about family. It was about community, too. Every woman who walked into the boutique left with more than lashes, shapewear, or brows. They left with encouragement. With a reminder that their scars didn't make them less beautiful. With proof that resilience could look glamorous.

Tanya's boutique had become more than a business—it was a testimony stitched into every conversation, every laugh, every hug.

Now, as she looked toward the future, Tanya understood the truth she had been carrying all along: survival wasn't the end of her story. Her story was about building something that would outlive her. Her boutique wasn't just hers—it was her daughters', her grandbabies', her community's.

When she thinks about legacy, *love* comes to mind. Not money, not property, not things. Legacy is love. Legacy is resilience. Legacy is standing in the ashes of your hardest day and saying, I'm still here.

And so are you!

Through pain, she had created purpose. Through battles, she had uncovered beauty. And through legacy, she had found peace.

And so can you!

The beauty lives on… Wherever you are, whatever you've faced, whatever you still carry—remember this: There is beauty in your battles, too.

Don't hide your scars or silence your story. Let your pain speak. Let it teach. Let it grow something new within you. For every broken piece you've ever gathered has shaped the masterpiece you're still becoming. Be gentle with yourself—you are both the storm and the sunlight that follows.

You are allowed to rest. You are allowed to heal. You are allowed to begin again, even here, even now. Because love never leaves us, and we must never leave ourselves.

Stand in your truth. Speak with courage. Walk with grace. And when you forget how far you've come, look at your own heart—still beating, still believing. That is where the beauty lives. Always.

But remember this, too—this is not the end. Tanya still has a lot of living to do and many dreams left to chase. There are chapters yet to be written, victories yet to be celebrated, and new beginnings waiting to unfold. The battles may have shaped her, but they will never define her.

Because every sunrise brings another chance—to rise higher, love deeper, and shine brighter. The story continues… and so does she!

19.　　Beauty in Battles

They say every storm runs out of rain. But nobody tells you how long you'll sit soaked in the aftermath. How long will it take for your bones to dry… How heavy healing really is…

This memoir—Tanya's memoir—isn't just about a building collapsing. It's about everything that tried to collapse within her. Pain didn't just break her bones—it questioned her purpose. The silence in that rubble? It was louder than any siren. But somewhere between being buried alive and being reborn on hospital sheets, she realized something…

I wasn't done yet. God didn't pull me out just to say "You made it." He pulled me out to say…

"Now show them what survival really looks like."

"Now walk—even if you limp."

"Now speak—even if your voice shakes."

"Now love—even with scarred skin."

"Now live—fully, fiercely, loudly."

And so she did, does, and will keep doing!

As Tanya approached her 50th birthday, a pivotal moment of reflection ignited a bold decision: to write this memoir. This milestone, steeped in both triumphs and tribulations, has inspired her to share her journey with authenticity and unapologetic honesty.

After weeks of writing in secret—late nights in her boutique, scribbling in her journal by candlelight—Tanya finally decided to share her story. Not with the world… not yet. First, she needed to share it with her girls.

It was a Sunday evening. The boutique was closed, but Tanya stayed behind. She was curled in her cheetah print chair, the air filled with the soft scent of burning sage and a flickering lavender candle. WBLS played in the background, low and soulful, as she rehearsed the words she'd written over and over again in her head.

When Ebony, her oldest daughter, stopped by to drop off a food container and give her a hug, Tanya handed her the worn notebook.

"What's this?" Ebony asked, eyes curious.

"My story," Tanya replied.

Ebony flipped through the first page, and within moments, her whole expression changed. The words pulled her in—the rawness, the strength, the humor, the pain. She was quiet for a long while, reading carefully, wiping her eyes when she thought Tanya wasn't looking.

When she finally finished, she looked up and said with a wide smile, "Mom… this is… so good. Like… really good. Wait—are you using our real names?"

Tanya chuckled. "Of course. It's our truth."

Ebony leaned back on the boutique's counter and shook her head in awe. "That's so dope, Ma. You've been through hell and back. This book? It's gonna speak to so many people. It already spoke to me."

That morning, Tanya read the back cover blurb aloud to her youngest daughter, Emani. They were on FaceTime, their usual early morning heart-to-heart space, before Emani went to work.

Tanya's voice was soft, but steady. "This is a story of **_Beauty In Battles_**—of a woman who was crushed, but not broken. Who lost everything and rebuilt with nothing but faith, grit, and a little bit of lip gloss. I am Tanya, and this is my story… in my own words."

By the time she reached the last line, Emani had tears streaming down her cheeks. "Mama…" she whispered, barely able to speak through the emotion. "That's… you. That's us. That's everything we've been through. You really wrote your book? Like for real? You go GURLL…!!'"

Tanya nodded, her own eyes full. "For real, baby."

Emani praised her, "I'm so proud of you. You're gonna help so many people. Women who've been through it—who thought they were finished. You're showing them they can come back stronger. Just like you did."

Then a few days later, Tanya was over at her little sister, Brianna's house, for a family gathering. She brought her notebook with her to share a page or two, nervous but excited. They sat in Brianna's kitchen over tequila shots and laughter, their usual rhythm.

Tamel, Dazjohn, Ebony, Mena, & Brianna at Ebony's wedding

"Bri, I want you to read this. It's just a draft… but it's my truth," Tanya said as she slid the notebook across the table.

Bri, curious as ever, flipped to the back first. That's when she read the blurb.

She read it twice.

Then she looked up with tears in her eyes. "Yo… this is so good. Like—this sounds like the back of a book I'd pick up at Barnes & Noble." She smiled through her emotion. "You should really publish this book, Tanya. I'm serious. I can't wait to read the whole thing."

She grabbed Tanya's hand and squeezed it. "Everybody's gonna want to read this. It's real. It's raw. And it's you. This is your STORY, sis."

In that moment, something clicked in Tanya. It wasn't just an idea anymore. It wasn't just pages in a notebook. It was a movement. A message. A ministry.

Her daughters saw it. Her sister felt it. Now… the world would be next.

Because when the people who know your heart say, "This is your truth," that's when you know—it's time to tell it loud. It's time to tell it proud. It's time to tell it… in your own words.

Crafting this narrative is not just an act of self-discovery; it's a way to connect with others who may find resonance in her experiences. With each page, she aims to capture the essence of resilience, growth, and the transformative power of embracing one's truth at this remarkable stage of life.

This story may sound like fiction to some, like a miracle to others. But to her? It's just *hers*. She has cried while writing and editing these pages, revisited pain that she tried to forget. She has peeled back the bandages—not to bleed again, but to prove she healed.

And she wants you to know this: If you're in your own battle, if life has knocked you down, buried you, or made you question if you'll ever smile again — Don't close the chapter. Don't quit on your becoming. Don't mistake the mess for the ending. There's beauty in every bruise, in every scar, in every shaky step you take toward wholeness. She found hers. And you will too.

Beauty in the mirror, the scars on her body tell a story that only the brave could survive. She used to hide them, ashamed of what they meant. But now… she sees them as medals—proof that battles have been fought and won.

Looking in the mirror now, she doesn't just see a woman who lived through a collapse… she sees a woman who rose through the rubble, even more powerful, more radiant, and unshaken. Beauty isn't what was lost. It's what was born from the fight.

Yes, there were days when the pain screamed louder than her thoughts. When she would lie in bed, staring at the ceiling, wondering if her body would ever feel like hers again, but she said no to hopelessness.

The surgeries left scars—not just on her skin but on her spirit. She couldn't bathe without assistance, couldn't sit up without wincing, and couldn't hold back tears when her children saw her like that. But that was just the surface. The deeper battle was within, facing the fear that she would never be the same woman again. Fear that the building hadn't just collapsed on her body, but on her confidence, her independence, her future. And yet, even in her darkest moments, there was beauty to be found.

Beauty came in the form of her daughter brushing her hair gently, whispering, "You still look like my mommy."

It came in the form of her partner, Stylist, massaging her hands each night, as if to remind her, *You are still here.*

It came in a mirror—one she avoided for weeks—until the day she looked in it and saw not a victim, but a warrior.

Tanya didn't overcome her battles all at once. It happened slowly, with quiet victories. The day she stood without help. The day she took three steps without collapsing. The first time she laughed again—really laughed—and didn't feel guilty for it.

She surrounded herself with love and refused to isolate in silence. She went to therapy. She prayed. She journaled. She yelled into pillows when it was too much. And then she got up and kept going. The most powerful beauty in her battle was rediscovering her purpose.

The building fell, but Tanya didn't. She realized she could use her voice and story to encourage other women— women who feel buried under life, trauma, or expectation. Through speaking engagements, community support, and Hotties Boutique, she started helping women reshape not just their bodies, but their lives.

Tanya didn't just survive—she rose. And in the end, her battle didn't take her beauty—it revealed it.

And not only this… a day before her 50th birthday party that her children gave her, she faced another significant loss, a tragedy unimaginable…

Turning 50 wasn't just another birthday for Tanya; it was a full-circle moment. A divine checkpoint. A milestone she almost didn't make it to.

There had been a time when she didn't know if she'd walk again, let alone celebrate another year of life. But here she was. Half a century of love, loss, lessons, and legacy— to commemorate this milestone, her four children got together and threw her a celebration. A wonderful one!

The birthday party was scheduled for April 12[th.] That same week, she called her father—her rock, her original cheerleader. "Daddy, you coming to my party, right?"

"Of course, Daughter. (That's what he called her) You know I wouldn't miss it," he said, voice raspy, full of love.

"You need help picking out what to wear?" she teased.

He laughed, quick and confident. "Daughter, don't play with me. I'm a fashionista too. I been fly before you were born. I got my whole look laid out."

She laughed too. "Alright, alright. I believe you. You better bring that energy."

Tanya with her Dad at the old boutique

That was Wednesday. By Friday night, everything changed…

She was at the UBS Arena, vibing to Mary J. Blige. Her cousin/friend Kenyatta had gotten her Mary J. Blige tickets for her birthday. They grew up on Morgan Ave. together.

During the intermission, Kenyatta presented her with a cake and cookies as a birthday present. The gesture was dope. It felt like the perfect kickoff to a celebration she'd earned.

But happiness was waiting to leave. Her phone rang. A call that split her in half. Her father—her superhero—was gone, just like that.

Tanya froze in the middle of the arena. The music became background noise. The glittery lights felt too bright. Mary's voice, usually her healing balm, suddenly felt like salt on an open wound. She wanted to run. To disappear into the night. To fall to her knees and cry for the man she called Daddy.

He was just fine. He was just picking out an outfit. He was supposed to be there…

Her chest hurt. Not the kind of pain a heating pad could fix. The kind that shook the soul.

"I don't want the party," she told her kids later that night through tears. "I can't do this. Not like this."

But Emani held her hand tight. "Mommy, you have to. You're still here. And this celebration is about you. We'll cry together later, but right now? Let us celebrate you."

Nonetheless, Tanya showed up. Heartbroken, but present. In a stunning emerald green dress that hugged her hips and flowed around her like royalty. Her face beat to perfection, her curls pinned up with silver accents. She looked like everything she had survived.

Everyone who mattered was there. Except her dear Daddy…

Tanya with her Daddy

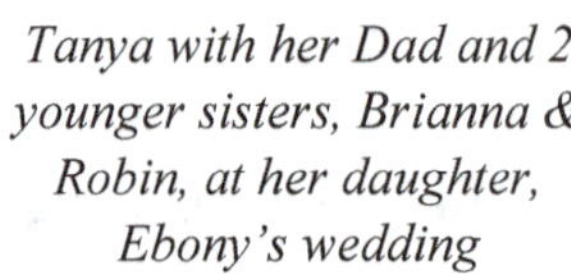

Tanya with her Dad and 2 younger sisters, Brianna & Robin, at her daughter, Ebony's wedding

Tanya's Dad at the time of COVID– 2020

The Tennis Club in Poughkeepsie was transformed into a dream: silver and emerald balloons, candlelit tables, white florals, and framed photos of her journey through the years—from baby girl to boutique boss.

The food was rich and soulful: baked salmon, seasoned rice, garlic string beans, mac and cheese, fried chicken, fresh rolls, and sweet tea. Cake that melts in your mouth.

The party was a big hit.

Her children and grandchildren were dancing and laughing. Her childhood friends. The women she'd met along the way. Customers turned family. People who had prayed for her, cried with her, and rooted for her when she was fighting for her life. Even with minor setbacks, even with last-minute changes—everyone who was meant to be there… showed up.

And that meant everything.

She stood near the end of the night, glass raised, voice trembling but strong.

"Tonight ain't what I planned. My Daddy was supposed to be here in his fly outfit, giving me that proud look he always did. But I know he's watching. I know he's smiling. And I know he's proud. This party… this life… this moment—is for him. It's for me. It's for all of us who keep pushing, even when our hearts break."

Tears fell. But there was laughter too. Hugs that healed. Music that uplifted. Love that overflowed. Fifty wasn't just a number. It was a badge of honor. A chapter Tanya almost didn't get to write. And that night, with swollen eyes, a glowing heart, and family by her side—she began writing the rest of her story, in her own words.

Turning 50

Tanya with 6 out of her 9 grandchildren
from left to right are: Amir, Coah, Kian, Kalai, Trinity, Teyani, &
bonus grandson Brent

Tanya's kids – she's in the back.
(I'll always have their backs no matter what)

Before closing her story, she wants to highlight something… ***"Her Girls"*** – the tribe that raised her.

Let's get one thing straight: She's definitely strong, but she didn't do it alone.

Behind every woman fighting battles is a tribe of real ones—ride-or-dies, the ones who hold your hand, cuss you out, pull you through, and pour you wine—all in the same breath.

Her friends are loud, wild, loving, messy, nurturing, crazy as hell, and beautiful. And they're truly hers.

Alberta – the style coach and dancefloor queen. Alberta came into her life when she was just 17— full of attitude, rhythm, and that bold confidence you couldn't help but admire. Alberta taught her how to walk into a room like she belonged there — even when she didn't feel like she did.

Tanya with Alberta's children, Shyeeka & Mariah

She was the first to drag Tanya to a real Jamaican party — bass thumping, hips whining rum in red cups — and she's been JAMACIAN ever since. (lol)

She showed her how to dress, helped shape the music she listened to (love me some reggae), how to move, and how to shine. When life tried to make her forget who she was, Alberta reminded her that she was still that woman — bold, beautiful, and never invisible.

Raquel – the forever BFF. She's her twin soul in a different body. She's been around forever. They've raised kids together like sister-wives without a husband. She was always about her hustle — always working, always stacking — while Tanya had the kids. While she was chasing the bag, Tanya was getting the crew off to school, as if it were her job. Anything Tanya needed, Raquel made sure she had it. (thank you)

But that's love — no keeping score, no counting favors. Pure love! Micah, her son, might've come from her, but he's a piece of Tanya's heart too.

Whenever she needed someone to talk to, someone to listen, or someone to offer words of encouragement or

Tanya & Micah

great advice (LOL), Tanya was there. (always will be) And when Tanya needs her, she shows up. That's sisterhood that doesn't fade.

Tasha – the glam squad and spiritual healer. She came from Queens with a flat iron in one hand and healing in the other. At first, it was just about hair — fresh sew-ins, sharp cuts, edges laid to perfection — but that chair turned into therapy. Over time, they became more than stylist and client; they became PNC.

Tasha and Tanya traveled, laughed, partied, and found joy in their freedom. But when life knocked Tanya down, Tasha didn't run. She came with fruit salad, bundles, and a flat iron. Her words that stitched Tanya's spirit back together: "Even when life's breaking you, sis, you still deserve to feel pretty." That stayed with her.

Aja – the work-friend who turned family. Tanya and Aja met at Saint Cabrini Home, both trying to survive the chaos of that place. Somewhere in the madness, God planted a friendship. She didn't have family nearby, and Tanya, being Tanya, stepped in. She started watching her son so she could work, and what started as babysitting turned into a bond that's lasted years.

Aja became Tanya's peace call — the one she'd hit up when life felt too heavy. "Aja, let's go," she'd say, and Aja'd pull up, lip gloss shining, ready to ride. They've laughed, cried, danced, and walked through storms side by side. Even though she was the last one Tanya met, it feels like she's known her forever — like their souls recognized each other long before they said *hello*.

Together, they are the beauty that held Tanya through the battles — the proof that sisterhood is the soft place God gives you to land when the world gets hard.

These women... are her **backbone.** They aren't just friends. They're chapters in her story, fingerprints on her healing, and co-authors of her joy. They've laughed 'til they peed, cried 'til their lashes fell off, fought and made up, loved hard, and survived even harder.

Every one of them showed up when it mattered—when the world got quiet, when Tanya felt like quitting, when she needed someone to see her behind the strength. They saw her, held her, and lifted her. Tanya loves them loud for it.

Epilogue

I was buried, but I did not die. I was broken, but I rebuilt. I was tested in ways I never imagined — physically, emotionally, spiritually — and I rose from it all, not just standing, but walking in purpose.

The battle didn't end when I left the hospital or put the cane down. Healing is layered, and some scars are invisible. But every day, I choose to show up — for my children, for my community, for every woman who's ever been told she couldn't, shouldn't, or wouldn't.

Beauty in Battles isn't just a title. It's a truth I live—a truth I earned.

So if you're reading this, carrying your own weight, your own wounds — know this: You are not alone, and you are not finished. Your story still has chapters waiting to be written. And if no one ever told you before, let me be the first...

You are the beauty.

You are the battle.

And you are the victory!

My truth is: beauty & battles will always live side by side. One shows you what you're made of; the other reminds you why you're still here. And after everything, I can finally say—I am both—the BEAUTY IN BATTLES.

When people ask me now how I kept going, how I kept laughing, kept dressing up, kept showing up—I tell them the truth…

"Because I'm not here just to survive. I'm here to remind you that beauty isn't what you see in the mirror—it's what you carry in your heart."

And now that this part of my story is written, the battles behind me… Just know—I'm already suiting up for the next one. Stronger. Wiser. Still standing. And still beautiful. With love, power, and purpose.

Rotanya… Your Comeback Queen 

My Heartbeat, My Why

To **my children** — Tamel, Dazjohn, Ebony, and Emani — my forever reasons, my living legacy. You are the rhythm that kept me going when the world went silent. Through every storm, every sleepless night, every moment I questioned my strength — your love pulled me back.

Watching you grow, stumble, rise, and shine has been the greatest gift of my life. You've seen me broken, rebuilding, and blooming again, and through it all, you loved me the same. You've taught me patience, purpose, and the kind of unconditional love that can only come from your own. You are my greatest battles and my most beautiful victories all at once.

To **my mother**, Gloria — my foundation, my quiet warrior. You are the voice that taught me resilience before I even knew what the word meant. You held me steady when life shook me, prayed for me when I couldn't pray for myself, and believed in me when I was running on fumes. Everything I am — the strength, the grace, the grit — it's a reflection of you. Thank you for being my anchor in every storm and my reminder that love doesn't give up.

And to **my love**, Stylist — my partner, my peace, my person. Thank you for standing beside me, not just in the sunshine but through every shadow. You've seen every version of me — the fire, the tears, the laughter, the fight — and you stayed. You've been my calm when life got loud and my strength when I felt weak. Thank you for choosing me, over and over again, even when the road wasn't easy.

To all of you — **my old & new family, my circle, my community, my heart** — thank you for all the prayers, calls, and visits… it wasn't in vain. Allah heard you. Thank you for walking this wild journey of life with me. Thank you for holding space for me through the trials, the triumphs, and everything in between. You are my flowers, and I give them to you now, with love and gratitude that words can't hold.

And just know this — that was only the beginning. We're not finished yet. The best is still unfolding…

Tanya's daughter's wedding
Her 2 sons, Tamel & Dazjohn
Her daughter, Emani
Herself & Stylist, along with
their fur baby, Nyla